· *Midnight Feast* ·

Martina Evans is a poet, and *Midnight Feast,* her first novel, introduces a bright new talent.

Born in 1961, the youngest of ten children, she grew up in County Cork and trained as a radiographer at St Vincent's Hospital, Dublin. In 1988, she moved from Eire to England, and went on to complete an honours degree in English and Philosophy at the Open University.

She now lives in north London with her husband, Declan, and her daughter, Líadáin. As a radiographer, she has worked in a prison and now works part-time in a hospital.

Her poems have been published widely in anthologies, magazines and newspapers, including the *Independent, Observer* and *New Statesman and Society*. Her first full-length collection of poetry, *The Iniscarra Bar and Cycle Rest,* was published by the Rockingham Press in May 1995.

MARTINA EVANS

· *Midnight Feast* ·

Mandarin

The author wishes to acknowledge her debt to
Women's Secret Disorder: A New Undertstanding of Bulimia
by Mira Dana and Marilyn Lawrence

A Mandarin Paperback
MIDNIGHT FEAST

First published in Great Britain 1996
by Sinclair-Stevenson
This edition published 1997
by Mandarin Paperbacks
an imprint of Reed International Books Ltd
Michelin House, 81 Fulham Road, London SW3 6RB
and Auckland, Melbourne, Singapore and Toronto

A CIP catalogue record for this title
is available from the British Library
ISBN 0 7493 2250 0

Phototypeset by Intype, London
Printed and bound in Great Britain
by Cox & Wyman Ltd, Reading, Berkshire

For all my girlfriends

It was in my mouth sweet as honey:
and as soon as I had eaten it,
my belly was bitter.

Revelation ch. 10, v. 10

· *One* ·

September 1977

My mother loved it. She could never get enough of it. And she got plenty of it, the night I arrived at Mayo.

I liked sympathy, too, but I didn't get much. And none from Sister Paul.

'Bringing up your daughter on your own. Without a man in the house and struggling against it all, to send her to the best of schools.'

'Well, it hasn't been easy.' My mother made a really pathetic effort to look modest.

'Easy! How could it be easy?' Sister Paul bellowed. 'You're a living saint, Mrs Jones. I said it to Sister Carmel this morning.'

Sister Paul fixed her grey eyes on me.

'And I hope *you* will be half the woman your mother is.' Her eyes were terrible. I wanted to look away, but I couldn't. I stared back and her two eyes seemed to fuse into one big lurid eye. Like Balor the Fomorian.

'Sit down, sit down. Sister Carmel is getting you tea.' Paul had a different voice for my mother. A creamy sympathetic one.

My mother was enjoying herself.

Footsteps came along the corridor. Too quick for a nun. They stopped and the door opened. I saw her.

Like a band of white light. Kneeling over her spilled luggage. Fair-haired. Fierce thin. Her eyebrows were like Spock's, except they didn't curl up at the ends as much as his did. Pulling the edges of the old bag together, she stuffed the clothes back. Small Sister Carmel had put the teatray down on the hall table and was trying to help. Tinny music was coming out of the blonde girl's pocket.

Sister Paul and my mother had their backs to the door. They couldn't see her. I stared down the V between their two bodies. She smiled at me. The way a boy would. Taking a long time.

'It's all right, Sister, I've got them now.' The girl pulled the bag away from Sister Carmel and ran off down the corridor.

Sister Paul and my mother turned around.

'What was that?' asked Sister Paul, her red mouth hanging open.

'A transistor radio,' Sister Carmel answered straight away. 'I told them to turn it off.'

'And who had the cheek and audacity to be playing a radio in the convent premises?'

'I don't know,' said Sister Carmel, her head bent over the tray as she put cups and saucers on the table. 'She wasn't wearing a uniform. It must have been one of the visitors.'

Sister Paul had a funny habit of pinching herself when she was thinking. She did it now, pulling out the pouch of a cheek. 'I thought I heard a familiar voice. I wonder, was she any relation to that MacSweeney girl? Oh, a troubled family! Let me tell you, Mrs Jones, the things we hear in this convent. We're like priests. We get all the problems.'

'Do you?' my mother asked, leaning closer.

'We do,' said Sister Paul and you could see that she was dying to tell. But I was there, so she couldn't.

Sister Carmel's tray was empty. She put it down and going to a small drawer took out a bundle of white damask table napkins. She put them on the table beside Paul and then stood with her small red hands folded at her waist.

'How is everything going?' Paul interrogated.

'Grand,' Sister Carmel said softly.

'And what about Mother Lorenzo's flower bed?'

'Sister Peter is clearing it up.'

'What a mess! I've never seen such pillage!'

I stiffened, feeling the back of my neck redden.

'It looks like some wild animal. There was talk of a fox seen on the farm,' Sister Carmel said, pursing her lips as if she was trying to be firm with Paul.

'Fox, my eye!' Paul interrupted. 'It was a human fox, as you well know.'

My mother bent over the silver spoons, examining them, running her fingers over them, feeling the design. If only she would own up. She was a continual embarrassment to me.

'Mr Cronin! I'm sure of it. He's so awkward. Who gave that man a Volvo?' asked Paul, in an outraged voice.

My mother lifted her head and darted me a look of pure triumph. She loved getting away with it.

'You'll have to excuse us, Mrs Jones,' Paul said, 'but we've had a flower bed ruined here tonight. Some vandal drove a car into it and broke all the railings. He didn't even have the gumption to own up. And we're all so upset. It belonged to Mother Lorenzo, she died only last year, the creature.'

'Ah, but, Sister Paul, you're talking to a woman who understands,' my mother said. 'Ask Grace. I'm just mad about flowers. I was admiring that lovely Mahonia Japonica. Well, I've never seen one look so good in September.'

'That's the one! You must have been the last person to see it in its glory.'

'Oh *no*!' My mother looked vicious. As if it was her flower bed that had been wrecked.

'Some parents!' sighed Sister Paul, 'You *know*, only that I can't say . . .'

'You don't have to tell me,' my mother said. 'I mean none of us is perfect but the *way* some parents . . .'

They couldn't say what some parents did. Their eyes met in impatient frustration, waiting for me to go.

I looked at Sister Carmel. Her eyes were lowered.

'I know the type.' My mother was chummy, patting Sister Paul's arm. '*Nouveau riche.*' She gave me another meaningful look, pleased with her success.

'There was a fox seen on the farm,' Sister Carmel persisted. 'Two chickens were found in a faint outside the henhouse . . .'

'Don't be bothering Mrs Jones now with talk about chickens,' Sister Paul cut in. 'Why don't you take Grace along to the convent refectory so that she can meet some of the other girls?' She turned to my mother. 'We always have a special tea in the convent for the girls, their first night back.'

'What a lovely idea. You're all so open here. The girls were never allowed into the convent in her old school.'

'What a beautiful mother you've got,' Paul said to me. 'You know you only look sixteen yourself, Mrs Jones, and how do you keep your hair so good? That lovely french roll.'

'Well, I can't afford a hairdresser,' my mother said in her self-sufficient voice, and threw a quick look at the sideboard mirror. 'Oh but your *skin*, Sister Paul, I've never seen anything like it.'

Sister Paul glanced in the mirror too before she denied it.

My mother forgot to kiss me. I know, because she jumped when I put my cheek against hers.

At the door, I looked back, but she was thick with Sister Paul. They were whispering already, 'Let me tell you . . .' 'The MacSweeneys . . .' and 'Isn't it, well, I know it . . .' And their eyes were round and their hands busy with jugs and sugar and silver spoons.

'Tell me, I'm like the grave,' my mother was saying, as Sister Carmel clicked the door softly behind us.

The refectory was full of girls. A long table covered with a white table cloth held cake and sandwiches. She was there. I could see the outline of her arms through her transparent white blouse. She was talking to two small girls. They looked like first-years. Their faces were full of admiration and I was jealous straight away.

Sister Carmel held my arm and guided me across the floor. 'We must find someone in your own year. Someone from Saint Joseph's dormitory.'

'Why Saint Joseph's?'

'That's where you'll be sleeping.'

Sister Carmel was moving towards her. I held my breath. She looked about my age. She knew we were coming. She stopped talking to the small girls and nudged the black-haired girl who stood beside her. I looked at her eyebrows again. She frowned and began to scrutinise mine. I thought I would die. I hated getting caught looking.

'Colette MacSweeney, she's in Saint Joseph's,' Sister Carmel half whispered to herself. 'And, of course, Patricia.'

'Who's your girlfriend?' Colette asked Sister Carmel and threw back her blonde hair. After winking at me.

'Stop that, Colette,' Sister Carmel said. 'This is the new fifth-year, Grace Jones. She's in Saint Joseph's with you.'

'I saw you in the convent parlour,' Colette said to me. 'You must be well in there.'

'I'm not!'

'It's all right, I don't mind.'

Colette put her hand on mine. It wasn't a pretty hand. It was kind of purple and pudgy. Not like her body. She was so thin. Her green woven sash was loose round her waist, almost sliding down her hips. Just managing to hang on.

Colette had a really cute way of squinting at you. 'I heard you were at the Ursulines before. Very grand.'

'It was okay.' I looked around for Sister Carmel, but she was gone across to the other side of the refectory. I saw her at a small table, lifting teapots. Looking serious through her square spectacles. Thinking about whether the teapots needed to be refilled.

'She's gone now,' said Colette, watching my face. As if I was going to be upset or something.

'It doesn't bother me,' I said.

'Carmel's all right.' Colette thought about it. 'No, I take that back. She isn't all right. She's a pain in the arse.'

'I'm Trish,' the other girl butted in quickly. 'Don't take any notice of Colette. Carmel's nice.'

'Where are you from?' Colette asked, adjusting my sash with her purple hands. 'You look sort of French.'

'Well, Carrignavar, actually,' I said, desperately flattered.

'It must be the thick eyebrows.' She pointed to Trish. 'She's got thick eyebrows too. I like thick eyebrows. Watch me eat ten slices of duck loaf in one hundred and eighty seconds,' she said suddenly, and started to stuff slices of the white iced fruity bread into her mouth.

I thought it was stupid. Juvenile. Like something you'd do when you were twelve. But I said nothing. It was nice watching her eyebrows, they kept going up. She wrinkled her forehead a lot. The two small first-years stared as well.

Colette threw down the last iced crust. 'Aren't you impressed?' she grinned at me, wiping her mouth with her hand and wiping her hand on her sleeve.

'Why?' asked Trish, lifting her short nose. 'Why should she be impressed?'

I couldn't say anything.

'Oh for Jesus sake!' Colette gave her a waspy look. 'I'm as sick as a dog now.' She staggered out of the room clutching her stomach.

'She's only looking for notice,' Trish said, offering me some duck loaf. 'It's her own fault. You should ignore half the things that Colette says.'

'Like what?'

'Like all this business about eyebrows, for instance. She's got a thing about them.'

'Has she?'

'Did you see her own?'

'Yeah, they're strange. But very nice.'

'She took the scissors to them when she was young and they've grown like that ever since.'

Sister Carmel came along again and Trish whirled round. The two sides of her straight black hair flew out like bats. 'Thanks for the duck loaf, Sister Carmel.'

Sister Carmel smiled and walked over to the first-years.

'She is very shy,' Trish said. 'But she is fierce nice. You should compare her to Mother Colm, who's a complete briar and only likes girls from West Cork! If you're not from anywhere west of Skibbereen you might as well forget it.'

Sister Carmel collected the empty plates and brushed crumbs from the table into her small puffed hands. The refectory door opened, and Sister Carmel ran forward to help a gaunt nun who came in, waving a shovel, full of earth, crushed yellow flowers and the splintered remains of delicate white paling. She was like something out of an Irish play. You'd expect her to make a speech about the ould sod. About the land that had been plundered. About the garden my mother had driven over.

'It's all right, Sister Peter,' Carmel said and helped her to carry the shovel and the earth into the kitchen.

Sister Peter wore the old-fashioned veil and her habit was lumpy and square. Carmel puffed around her, soft and round. She didn't seem to mind the earth that Sister Peter had spilled over her clean habit. Or the cakes of mud that the first-years ground into the floor as they ran out of the refectory. When all the buns were gone.

· Two ·

Trish wasn't too bad once you got to know her. She was definitely more reliable than Colette. Too reliable. She was always there. Sometimes she seemed to read my mind.

'The very worst thing, here, is if you get caught in another girl's bed,' Trish announced, kneeling on my bed.

'That's stupid,' I said and hoped my face hadn't gone red.

'Well, they go absolutely berserk. It's the world's worst according to them.' Trish's voice dropped lower and a gust of wind muttered at the door.

We were in Saint Joseph's dormitory. The dormitory was where we always went. And Mother Colm was always chasing us out. She said it was unhealthy. That we should be having brisk walks in the open air, to drive oxygen to our brains and air to our souls. But I preferred to lie on my bed and read novels.

Trish always came to look for me. But this time it wasn't even four o'clock. This was our morning break. I could hardly keep my eyes open during first class. I had been up late every night with Colette for a week.

Colette was okay. She just skipped Mass and slept in.

I tried to skip Mass too, but Paul came to look for me the very first morning I dodged.

'You're too new, too noticeable,' Colette said, without sympathy. 'You're supposed to be a brainbox, I heard them talking. They're probably afraid if you don't go to Mass you'll stop studying.'

But I wasn't able to study either. I kept on reading novels. Thinking, I'll stop now after this one. And then I'd find another book and it would go on and on. Novels were drugs. I was devoted to them. Covering them carefully with brown paper, smuggling them into study. Colette was a kind of a novel, too. A novel on long thin legs.

'You'll have to try to get more sleep,' Trish went on as I lay on my bed and yawned and yawned. I looked at the ceiling. The paint was peeling here and there, and the uneven appearance gave rise to shapes. Rabbits and dogs, a vicious face with a long nose. I closed my eyes.

'Trish?'

'What?'

'Do you know what I'd really like?'

'No.'

'To be stretched on a rack. I'm so tired, I can't even stretch when I yawn. I'd love if someone could stretch me.'

'Do you want me to try?'

'Okay.' I opened my eyes, surprised that she was taking me seriously.

'You hold on to the bars at the head of the bed and I'll pull your feet.'

'Right.'

I gripped the iron bars and Trish pulled.

It was really brilliant. I could feel my muscles

unwrinkling. A lovely pain worked its way into all the numb crevices.

'Harder, harder,' I said.

'Jesus, I can't go any harder,' Trish gasped.

'Oh yeah, that's great. Put me on the rack. I can take it.' Trish's hands slipped and slithered on my ankles. I could feel her losing her grip.

'Do you want me to do it to you, now?' I asked. I got up and gave a little gasp of surprise at Mother Colm who had suddenly appeared at the foot of the bed like a bad dream.

'And what may I ask are two girls doing lumping around on the beds at half past ten on a Friday morning?'

'Mother, I was just . . .'

'Well you can take that "just" out of your vocabulary, firstly.' Mother Colm stuck her lower lip out importantly. 'Now tell me what you were doing.'

'We came upstairs and I was just . . .'

'Stop right there! Can you not speak without using that word?'

'No, Mother, I came up here with Grace because I,' Trish's lips trembled on the ghost of another 'just', 'needed pencils.'

'And what was the connection between getting your pencil and vandalising the furniture?'

'We weren't vandalising the furniture.'

'Throwing your big bodies around those beds. Beds are for sleeping.'

'My pencil fell down behind the head of the bed and Trish was holding my ankles in case I fell.'

'You're such a Slim Jim, I suppose. That you'd fall through those bars.'

'We were taking no chances.'

'God give me patience!' Mother Colm roared. 'Is that the command of English you can manage after three years of the Ursulines? I wouldn't believe it, only I'm hearing it with my own ears.'

'Mother, Grace had no pencil and I brought her up here because I've a few spare ones in my locker,' Trish said, fiddling with a piece of her hair.

'And,' Colm's eyes bored into Trish, 'I suppose you needed her to help you up the stairs. A big strong over-developed girl like yourself, could you not mount the stairs alone?'

Trish went red.

Colm gave her an irritated look. 'And take your hand down from your hair. How many times do I have to speak to you about that dirty habit!'

While Colm looked at Trish, I picked up two pencils from my locker. Trish dropped her hair and, glancing back at Colm, she made a move to go.

'What are you waiting for?' Colm bellowed and we fled to the big wooden door at the end of the dormitory.

We ran down the middle corridor, conscious as we went of Colm's footsteps. The corridor was dark. It had a low ceiling. There were statues in alcoves along the way. With pink and shadowy faces. Spooky.

The geography lab door opened suddenly and made us jump. A girl came out. She wore a grey polo-necked jumper and glasses. She had long brown hair plastered down her cheeks.

'Noreen O'Donovan, I've been looking for you everywhere!' Mother Colm's voice softened. 'When are you coming to see me about your Irish oral?'

Noreen O'Donovan was not only from West Cork, she was a native Irish speaker. Mother Colm loved her. They were always going off together for private tutorials and Irish sessions.

'You look a bit tired,' Colm said. 'That grey jumper is draining you. You know if I was your mother, I'd dress you always in cream and brown.' Colm stepped back to get a full view of Noreen. 'You should always wear your hair to the side, your face is away too small and dotey for that middle crease.'

Noreen and Mother Colm began to talk in Irish. And we kept going. I hated Mother Colm. I hated being stuck with a stupid excuse.

'I should have said you were massaging my ankles.'

'Shh,' said Trish.

I heard Mother Colm's voice behind me. 'What are you saying now?' She waddled up determinedly. 'I'm going to get on to Sister Paul about you.' Her voice tagged along after us, 'Yes, I'm still here. I'll say no more for the moment, Miss Jones, but I'll be watching you.' She went off towards the convent, the heels of her small black shoes clacking on the floor. I had hardly arrived and I was getting into trouble.

Colette was furious. She stood at the open door of the classroom, her hands on her hips, fingering the coloured woven sash that snaked around her waist. Her slanty green eyes were cold stones and she directed all her anger at me.

'That's really thick getting caught in the dormitory. Colm will be after you all the time now.'

'I'm sorry,' I said, feeling foolish. 'It's all my fault. Don't blame Trish.'

'Oh God, you're so pathetic. It's all my fault,' Colette mimicked mockingly. 'You won't be able to fart now, but the nuns will be around with sound detectors.'

She swished back her silky blonde hair, and disappeared into the classroom. And sat at her desk with her head turned away from me. I sat down and opened my maths book.

Paul was coming at eleven to 'introduce' us to honours maths. She came in a rush and took over the room immediately with her big pale body. Saying the Hail Mary as if it were the national anthem. Making the sign of the cross as if it was a salute, her long white hands firmly touching brow, shoulders and breast. I looked at Colette. Her hands were joined, her head bowed. She was ignoring me.

Sister Paul gave all the girls in the front row a glassy look. I shifted my feet uncomfortably. I had a desperate itch between my shoulder blades. I shrugged uneasily, waiting for it to pass.

Without warning, Paul said to Noreen O'Donovan, 'What is integration?'

Noreen, surprised, said she didn't know.

'You see!' said Paul, 'You're lying on top of these desks as if it is a holiday camp. Well it's not! Twenty-four girls got the call to National Teaching last year. This is not a place for idleness. Noreen O'Donovan, your sister is below in that leaving cert classroom and, if she heard the answer that you've given me today, she'd bow her head in shame.'

'I wasn't ready,' protested Noreen feebly.

'You weren't ready? What kind of answer is that? Education is something you carry with you and I intend that every girl here carries their education with them. If I meet any girl here, whether it be on their way to Mass or on the volleyball court or during their summer holidays, I will say to that girl, what is integration? and I will expect that girl to know the answer. That's what education is!'

Sister Paul was pleased that we were so bad. She fixed her close-set eyes on the class. Her eyes joined up. She was Balor the Fomorian again. Everybody knew she was going to ask somebody else what integration was and everybody hoped it wasn't going to be her.

'Aine Colbert, tell me what integration is?' Paul

adopted a confidential tone as if she was enquiring after the girl's health.

'I don't know, Sister.'

Sister Paul went around the classroom, but not one girl could define it. Nobody was going to own up to knowing about integration now, it was too controversial.

'Grace Jones, do you mean to tell me that you do not know what integration is?'

'Not really, Sister.'

'Not really! Does that mean you have some idea what it is?'

'Oh no, Sister.'

'Is it so shocking to know about integration? Grace, you seem shocked that I might suggest such a thing?'

'No, Sister. I'm very sorry, Sister.'

Paul stood up straight and gazed out of the window, wistfully. 'Those poor Ursuline sisters, thanks be to God they can't hear you. Those poor creatures.' She turned back to me, with a savage look in her eye. 'How could you let down your old school like that? I'd never have expected it from an Ursuline boarder.'

She told us to take out our books and look up the answer. Sitting down squarely on the high chair, she took out a black missal. We sank our heads and the clock ticked louder. Sounds drifted from the next classroom. The first-years were saying their French verbs, '*Je suis, tu est, il est.*' Squeaky high cartoon voices. I stared at the wavy integration curve. Maybe I should give up honours maths.

At the end of the class, Paul asked, 'Do you all know what integration is now?'

'Yes, Sister.'

'Well, you can tell Miss Kingston. She'll be taking you tomorrow for maths, biology and chemistry. She's your teacher for the rest of the year.'

Paul stood up and shut her missal sharply. 'And get those big lazy bodies off those desks, you're like fat cats rolled up in yourselves. Posture, posture, if you please! Come on, now! Shoulders back and squared, chins parallel to the floor, knees perpendicular. Order, order in everything, if you please.'

She swept to her feet, palming her forehead importantly. 'In the name of the Father, the Son and the Holy Ghost, Amen.'

When Paul had left the classroom, Colette started talking to me again and, although I was annoyed with her, I couldn't help talking back. It was like that with me and Colette.

· *Three* ·

Friday's lunch was awful. Fish in breadcrumbs swimming in grease. I thought that it was desperate that Carmel had to handle such horrible dinners.

'She loves it,' Colette said. 'She wants to suffer.'

And Carmel went on serving dinners, looking saintly, with her head bent.

Trish was worried. 'What if Colm tells Paul? It's the worst thing, getting caught in bed.'

'But we weren't really in bed.'

'You were, you were,' Colette chanted, beating her spoon on the table.

'Shh,' I said, as Carmel came by, carrying a stack of stainless-steel dish covers.

'Well, you've only got yourselves to blame,' said Colette, and lifted her sardonic eyebrows. 'Do have some more of these delicious cod-flavoured carrots?'

'I can't bear to look at it. I've got a Scrumble bar in my locker for afterwards. Don't put me off it.'

'How many more have you got?' Colette asked, pretending to be astounded. 'You've been eating them all bloody week.'

'Try and eat your dinner,' Trish said.

'Don't eat your dinner,' ordered Colette. 'And don't eat the Scrumble bar. You're too fat.'

'Don't be stupid,' snapped Trish, looking wildly mad at Colette.

'Oh, you just want her to get fat, don't you? Because then I won't love her any more. You are so jealous.' Colette stared at Trish with slitty eyes.

'Stop it for God's sake,' I said, but I was really thrilled.

Carmel rang the gong for Grace After Meals and we all got up from our seats. I stood very straight and tried to look as if I just happened to be sitting next to Colette. As if I had nothing to do with all the noise and shouting.

'Look,' lectured Colette, as we were leaving the refectory, 'you can have that Scrumble bar if you promise to run round the walks ten times after school.'

'It's too cold.'

'You won't be cold when you're running and we'll come with you.' Colette grabbed Trish by the arm and pressed her face against Trish's shoulder. 'We don't mind at all, do we, Trish? Anything to keep Grace looking beautiful. What do you think?'

I gave in. Even though I hated running, it would be different with Colette. And Colette was pleased too. She put her purple fingers inside my belt and tickled my waist as we made our way to the classroom after our lunch.

On my desk, I had built a nest of books. That's where I hid the open pages of my novel. Today I was reading *The Tenant of Wildfell Hall.* The teachers didn't notice. Most of them were kind of gentle with me, because I was new. Because I was supposed to be a good student. I had ten honours in the Inter. But that meant nothing. I had a feeling that they were going to get wise to me soon. I would have to stop reading novels in class. But not yet. Only fifty more pages to go now. I read on through double French.

Running round the walks wasn't too bad. I didn't get caught for breath. The air in my throat was only just beginning to go sweet, when my legs gave out. I sat down in front of Our Lady's grotto and waited for Colette and Trish to finish. Colette was the last to give in. After five and a half laps.

'I'm never going to be a virgin,' she gasped, sprawling on the ground in front of the grotto.

'That doesn't make sense,' Trish said, pulling at her black fringe.

'Shut up, you're only a virgin yourself.'

'So are you.'

'That's what you think!' Colette said. And it didn't sound like bravado. She had an air about her. Of seriousness. We were silent for a few minutes. The breeze got sharper, the clouds got lower. She had a habit of ruining things and it seemed to affect the weather.

'But anyway you can't become a virgin in the future. That's what it sounded like when you said it. You can be one in the beginning, but you can't become one,' Trish tried hard to be ordinary and logical.

Colette's face closed up, 'Oh you know best, Trish. We all know that you're *so* experienced.' She put on a far-away look and stared at a heap of trees that were clutching onto each other at the bottom of the walks. 'It's time to go.'

We followed her down the walks and in the side door of the cloister.

Mother Colm was waiting, with her lips stuck out majestically.

'Mrs Joyce and Miss Pole have come all the way from the City to give you drama and elocution lessons.

Kindly have the courtesy to be on time.' She glared at me and Trish.

'I have to wash, I'm stinking,' Colette wrinkled her nose and fanned her face with her hand. As if Colm wasn't there at all.

It annoyed me, the way Colette didn't seem to care if I got into trouble. Colm kept staring at me as if I was the cause of everything.

Colette tried to chase me up the brass staircase, but I refused to run. Stomped up one at a time. Trish walked beside me, muttering, 'Oh no, oh God. We're in for it. She'll get us yet.'

'Ignore her,' Colette slowed down and hovered impatiently beside us. 'I just feel sorry for anyone with a backside that size. You should see her bloomers.'

'Yeah, well it's okay for you,' Trish replied. 'My fees have been specially reduced because my father couldn't afford them this year.'

My stomach began to separate itself into cold slices. I knew what my mother had been up to in the convent parlour. Talking about her reduced circumstances.

'They never let you forget it. Not ever. Do you remember last year when Rosario said to Noreen O'Donovan that she didn't need to pay her music fees? In front of the whole school! Do you remember her smarmy look, saying, "Sure we wouldn't expect any money from you and your parents trying to scrape the price of the fees together"?'

'Isn't your mother a widow?' Colette asked me. 'Jesus, you'll be getting away with murder. Free laundry and everything, I suppose.' She punched my arm playfully.

We kind of cheered up, then, and after we had washed our hands, Colette sprayed us all with a strong perfume called Nitelife. We wafted down the stairs.

As we passed some of the leaving certs clustered on

the middle corridor, one of them said: 'Who's wearing the flyspray?'

'Don't take any notice,' Colette said. 'They're only jealous.'

Stopping in front of Our Lady's altar, Colette undulated from side to side, her slanted eyes closed, as she twirled her multi-coloured woven sash. She turned round and shouted at the leaving certs, 'Belly dancing! Belly dancing!'

The leaving certs glared, speechless. Some of them turned away and ignored Colette. They wouldn't give her the soot of it. Others didn't have the self control.

'You think you're so smart, Colette MacSweeney,' one of them said, finally, and Colette laughed, delighted. She ran off down the stairs ahead of us, shaking her hair wildly.

We walked along the lower corridor, walking alternately on black and then white tiles. The refectory door was open and Sister Carmel was putting butter dishes on the tables. The sun was shining on her small kittenish figure as she cut the bright yellow butter into slices. Sister Carmel had the smallest feet I'd ever seen. They were like little tufts. It seemed cruel to have them laced into hard black nun's shoes.

'*There is a house in New Orleans they call the rising sun, and it's been the ruin of many a poor boy,*' Colette sang in a very deep voice and Sister Carmel nodded shyly. '*God knows, I know, I'm one.*' Colette kept singing.

Carmel put her finger to her lips. 'Don't be so loud! You'll upset Mother Colm.' But, she looked only half annoyed when she walked off towards the pantry.

Colm was waiting for us outside the study door.

'What are you doing, Grace Jones, wearing those mad purple socks? The syllabus states clearly that it's bottle-green socks for weekdays and white socks for Sundays. Did you not know that?'

'Well, I did, Sister, but I just thought that these ones were okay because they were a present from my aunt.'

'And who is your aunt to be telling us what the girls of this school should be wearing?' Colm raised her voice. 'Go up the stairs this instant and put on the correct socks,' she thundered. 'And before you go, don't let me hear you using that American slang word, okay, again. You'll speak correct English while you're in this school. I don't know what you learnt at the Ursulines.'

She was making me late for class. I waited to see if Colm relented but she shouted about disobedience and I hurried up the stairs. When I got out of sight I took two steps at a time.

'And *who* is your aunt?' her words echoed up the stairs after me. Colm probably thought my aunt too was a poor widow. She was a widow all right. But a rich one.

'I'd never beg. I'd never ask for anything,' my mother always said. But I knew that she asked Auntie Catherine for loads of things. I liked Auntie Catherine and Delia my cousin. I often wondered why I liked Delia when she was so perfect. Maybe it was because she was always nice to me. Maybe I felt I had to, because my mother preferred Delia to me, and I was ashamed that I wasn't the preferred one.

I arrived in the dormitory, my legs shaking with exertion and when I tried to put on my socks standing up, I wobbled all over the place. I sat on the bed and waited for the drumming pulsations in my legs to subside. By the time the muscles stopped beating, I was ten minutes late.

Mrs Joyce was speaking when I pushed open the study door. She was a shortish woman with a dark mahogany tan and she wore a tight-fitting white dress squeezed at the waist with a wide black patent leather belt. She barely nodded when I excused myself, simply indicated that I should join the circle of girls gathered around her.

I squeezed myself in between Trish and Colette. Mrs Joyce had a thin little smile on her face. 'I'm taking all your names. What's yours?'

'Grace Jones.'

'Grace, we were just talking about *Deirdre of the Sorrows*, do you know that story?'

'Yes.'

'Does everybody here know that story?' Most girls nodded. 'Well, if you don't, you must get Grace here to tell you. You mustn't forget our Irish legends, we have a very rich cultural heritage.'

'For God's sake, tell me, I'm dying to be cultured,' Colette whispered, pretending to be panicking about it.

Mrs Joyce used dramatic hand movements as she spoke, sheathing and unsheathing her long red finger nails, opening and closing her fists. She spoke in the same exaggerated manner, her mouth like a pair of scissors, clipping and cutting her words. And yet she seemed to be tired, her dark eyes very old in her smooth tanned face.

She paused wearily, 'Where was I? Oh yes, I think I've got all your names now. Miss Pole is going to talk to you about *The Merchant of Venice.* I'll hand you over to her, now.' She finished, plunging her hands through the air, as if they were knives cutting through the jungle.

'A trained actress, of course,' Colette whispered. 'Wouldn't you know! She'll cut someone one of these days with those bloody daggers of nails.'

Miss Pole got up from her seat in the corner and made big steps to the centre of the room. She was tall and fierce thin, dressed completely in purple. Her purple trousers were tight and she wore them tucked into purple suede boots. Everybody stared at Miss Pole, while Mrs Joyce sat down and wrote in a navy-covered book.

Miss Pole spoke about drama during Shakespeare's time and read Portia's speech on the quality of mercy while we all looked at her thighs. Her voice was lower than Mrs Joyce's.

Mrs Joyce then gave a short talk on vowel sounds and some tongue twisters to practise our 'th' sounds. She did horrible exercises with her tongue, turning it sideways and rolling it up like a carpet. Trish could turn her tongue sideways and Colette could roll hers up. I could do neither.

When it was time for them to go, our eyes followed Miss Pole's purple legs to the door. She was so thin.

· *Four* ·

Mrs Joyce and Miss Pole stalked out on their high heels at six thirty. Tall, dignified people. Worlds away from us. They left me feeling awful shabby. And I thought that was strange, because I wouldn't want to be like them in the least.

When the door had shut behind them, the noise started up. Dreary noise. I swayed on my feet, feeling trance-like. The orange plastic chairs were dragged, scraped and stacked away. We went down to the other end of the study and there was Colm waiting at the stained-glass door.

'Single file, if you please. Make your way quietly to the refectory.' She stared at socks as each girl walked past.

Outside on the corridor, two first-years made their way to the refectory. Slowly, languidly, their arms draped around one another. One of them was noticeable, with thin legs, a short gymslip and frizzy red hair.

'Hi!' roared Colm, catching sight of them. She ran away down the corridor behind them. 'Stop there, this instant! You, you, yes, you. I'm talking to you. You, with the bold red hair.'

'Me?'

'Separate yourself, immediately.'

The two first-years had gone as red as anything, but still Colm went on and on. 'A filthy habit! Don't let me see it again!'

'Gotta get outa here, man,' Colette said and led us past the outraged Colm.

'Those poor things!' I was really savage about Colm.

'Well, that's what it's like here, girl,' Colette said in her woman of the world voice. 'You just thank God it isn't yourself that's getting it.'

'But you don't even care,' Trish said.

'That is true,' Colette said in a very serious thoughtful voice. And then roared at the top of her lungs, 'I don't give one fucking damn!'

'Colm'll hear you,' said Trish, biting her nail, looking embarrassed.

'She hears nothing. She's a fat fool and her ears are full of wax. Did you ever see them?'

'No,' I said, quickly.

'They're full of it. Yellow, sticky, concentrated, consecrated . . .'

'Please stop!'

'Yes,' said Trish. 'You'll put us off our tea.'

'I should have known that you'd be worried about that!'

'What's for tea?' I interrupted.

'Well I certainly don't care. I have had my fill of duck loaf. And furthermore,' Colette continued, 'did you see Miss Pole?'

'She is so thin.'

'She's perfect.'

'I'd love to be that skinny,' Trish ran her hands down her thighs as if she could rub them away.

'Well, you won't be if you continue on the way you're

eating,' Colette said. 'I'm never going to eat duck loaf again. It's about seven thousand calories a slice.'

'It's not!' I was shocked.

'Duck loaf is just pure fat!' Colette insisted. 'And the icing is just pure sugar. There's a quarter pound of sugar in every slice.'

We were very quiet as we walked down the corridor, thinking about duck loaf. The sun beamed in the big windows, and covered us in light. Colette shook her fair hair, it was really brilliant. It made her look like a pure angel. My legs felt heavy, I went into another trance. I held on to it carefully, letting the sunlight coat me all over. I would have liked that corridor to last for ever. Colette put her hand on my shoulder and I shivered.

A group of girls suddenly raced past us, making an awful racket. Colette dropped her hand from my shoulder. Everything was suddenly sharp and cold.

'Wait, what is it?' I shouted.

But Colette was gone. Running like a man. Powerful steps. Girls cleared a cone shape in the crowd to let her pass. Then some leaving certs thundered past. We could hear shrieks and cries coming from the refectory.

'What is it?' I asked Trish.

'There's buns for tea,' a straggling leaving cert gasped, and then made an extra spurt to keep ahead.

'Quick!' shouted Trish. 'We have to be quick.'

I wished that I didn't have to run. I was tired. Disappointed because my trance had left me, I wanted to lie down. But I didn't stop. It was worse to be left behind.

The refectory door was locked. A large crowd of girls stood pressing themselves against the big wooden door. We couldn't get near Colette, who stood about five deep.

She turned round and shouted, 'There's buns for tea!'

'We know,' said Trish, annoyed that Colette was so far ahead.

There was the sound of clattering dishes from the refectory, but the door remained shut. The girls stared into the dark wood, as if they could look the door open. The waiting crowd got more anxious and pressed tighter while those at the head of the queue turned round, irritated and squashed, and said, 'Take it easy for God's sake!'

Trish said that there were never enough buns to go round and some savages tried to steal two. 'Poor old Carmel, she isn't able for it, you know.'

A girl beside me took out her locker key, and began cleaning her nails with it, digging out the dirt, examining it as if it was science. At that moment, I hated Mayo. I hated that dim corner outside the refectory door, squashed so close to the girl in front of me, that I could hear her breathe, see the mistake in the neck of her hand-knitted jumper. I hated Colette with her long legs and Trish with her hair so straight it never needed combing. And I was sick of Colette being a smart arse. I saw her at the head of the queue, swishing her blonde hair. Winking at me. I didn't look at her.

And then the refectory door opened and the noise rose up. Everybody pushed, shoved and squeezed through the narrow opening. Girls banged on either side of the door and screamed in outrage at the successful. Sister Carmel staggered back, holding onto her veil as everyone charged through. The heavy refectory door crashed against the wall and Sister Carmel fell against it weakly saying, 'Girls! Girls!'

'It's always the same, blood hungry hounds,' Colette said, giving a good hard push to the girl in front of her.

We were all swept forward and as we flowed with the crowd, I could see Colette coming out the other side. Holding a large cream horn high above her shoulder.

When we got to the table there was no time to linger over the choices. You just had to grab quickly and run over to the counter where Sister Peter was pouring cups of tea. I got a little white iced bun with a cherry on top. It was not a bun I would have freely chosen and someone knocked off the cherry as I was making my getaway.

The crowd slowed down then, as the news that 'All the buns are gone!' filtered through. The last of the girls trudged in and made do with bread and butter. With sour faces.

'I think I'll start that diet tomorrow,' Colette said, grinning as with a curvy, nasty looking stainless steel fork she stole some cream from Trish's bun.

'Where did you get that fork?' Trish asked crossly, holding her doughnut against her chest.

'Testy, testy!' Colette said, lightly. 'I only took a tiny bit, look have some of mine.'

'That's artificial cream.' Trish looked scornfully at Colette's cream horn and swallowed down the end of her bun. She pointed to the door at the end of the refectory. 'That's the door that's never opened.'

'Why?' I asked.

Trish shrugged her shoulders, but Colette butted in quickly, 'There's a dead nun walled up behind it with her illegitimate triplets.'

'Pull the other leg,' I said, half-wishing that Trish would say it was really true.

'That's blasphemy!' Trish said, severely, to Colette.

'Go 'way, you. You're only mad because I took the cream from your bun.' Colette laughed and then put on Sister Paul's deep voice. 'Selfish, selfish girl, Our Lady is crying to see your greed.'

Sister Peter went past, carrying a bunch of empty teapots in each hand. She still looked like someone from an Irish play. Now she looked like one of those tortured mothers whose only son had been killed by the Black and Tans. Or taken by the sea. I expected her to say, 'Ah Seanie, Seanie, where are you now, with the sea closed over your head?' or 'Packy, Packy, what have I done to be told that they found you like this? Thrown in a ditch with a bullet in your head?'

I nudged Colette to tell her.

'I can't kiss you now. Not with my mouth full,' Colette said, holding her purple hand high in the air.

Sister Peter heard Colette as she came back with the full teapot. A look of horror passed across her wise and tortured features. 'Jesus, Mary and Saint Joseph, tonight.' Sister Peter said and then looked even sicker when she realised that she'd said it in front of us.

We kept our faces kind of straight while she passed and then Colette said in a country accent, 'Jesus, Mary and Saint Joseph and the Donkey, tonight!'

'I thought she was going to bless herself when she looked at Colette,' Trish said.

'We'll all be in trouble, now,' I said, half thinking that it was fairer that way.

'That nun is afraid of me,' Colette said airily.

Sister Carmel had managed to get back to her place by the buffet table. Holding her head stiffly as if she was afraid her veil might fall off. She looked relieved to see that all the buns were gone. As more girls came in, she offered them bread and butter. Some of them weren't very nice about it.

Sister Peter went up the refectory again with more empty teapots and Colette rushed after her.

'Can I give you a hand, Sister?'

Sister Peter didn't answer, just hung on tightly to her teapots.

'Ah, please, just one. Won't you let me help you?' Colette said in a seductive devil voice.

'I'm all right,' said Sister Peter and clattered off.

'You shouldn't tease her,' Trish said, when Colette came swaggering back to us.

'I was not teasing her. I was offering to help. Wasn't I, my love?' Colette raised her Spock eyebrows at me.

'I don't know what you were doing,' I said. I was feeling a bit disgusted with Colette.

We stood for a moment in silence and then Trish burst out: 'It's fine for you, Colette. Your family has buckets of money. The nuns wouldn't say a word to you. They're afraid they might lose a share in your father's millions. What about us?'

'He's only got about one million, the eedjit,' Colette said, grinning.

'You make me sick! Why don't you do it to Paul, if you're that smart? Oh God, just imagine. Taking advantage of poor old Peter!'

'Look I'm sorry about Peter, it just seemed funny that's all! But you shouldn't take it out on me because my father is rich. You know I'm a Communist.'

'Ah, Communist my arse!' said Trish savagely.

'Well, at least *you've* got a nice family,' Colette said, her voice gone wobbly all of a sudden.

'Your mother is nice enough. She's got a lovely tan,' Trish said.

'Yeah, but my father is awful. Johnny says he's a gangster, and anyway . . .'

'Anyway what?'

'Johnny is really hard on me.'

'I thought you were mad about your brother Johnny,' I said, trying to coax Colette out of this mood. She was about to cry.

'I am, but he's a bully. He makes me do everything he wants.'

Trish's face looked awful. Mine probably looked awful too. I wanted Colette to stop talking. And I wanted her to go on. I wanted her to cry and yet I knew I'd hate it if she did. I put my arm around her waist. Her purple hands fluttered on top of mine. I felt I was the strong one. Colette covered her face with her hands. And then suddenly looked up, wiping her hands on her gymslip. Laughing like mad.

'Fooled ye!'

'You didn't fool us at all,' said Trish crossly, and Carmel was ringing a little bell. To get rid of us, so that they could clean up. Colette went out singing.

We passed Sister Peter who was shining knives at a small table.

'Goodbye, Sister,' Colette said. Sister Peter shuddered and kept shining with her head down.

'Look how nice I really am,' Colette said, refusing to admit defeat. 'You can't break it off with me now.' She stood there with her hands pressing against her blonde fringe. Wouldn't move until I put my hand around her waist. I could see Colm peering from the other end of the corridor. I managed to drag Colette away from Colm's view but not before Colette said, 'You're not ashamed of our relationship, are you?' In a really loud voice.

· *Five* ·

I gave Colette half of my orange and asked her was she all right.

'Why wouldn't I be all right?' Colette said. 'You're really mental sometimes. I just want to dance, baby.'

'Dance?'

'Yeah, it's recreation at nine and we're going to get out the old records.'

'Records?'

'Look,' Colette put her hands on either side of my head and got me to look at the old record player sitting on top of a tall wooden table. 'We're going to get that weight off your hips, girl.'

'Are the records any good?'

'Absolutely desperate. The worst I've ever seen. They're so bad they're good. They have *Little Arrows.* Imagine!'

'What's *Little Arrows?*'

'It came out when you were barely out of the cradle.'

'Why don't people bring their own?'

'Because they'd get all scratched.'

'The girls used to bring their own records at my last school.'

'Look, girl, I couldn't bring in my records. The nuns would have heart attacks.'

'Why?'

'My records are fucking mad. Johnny picks them out for me.'

'Why do you let him?'

'Because he's got really brilliant taste,' Colette snapped. 'He knows everything about records and I want to learn about everything.'

'So do I.'

'No, you don't.'

'I do.'

'Well why don't you let me touch you?'

'I do.'

'You don't, well not properly anyway.'

'What kind of records have you got?'

'Well, I've the Sex Pistols . . .' Colette stopped for an effect. She got it. I went red. 'Are you sure that they're a real band?'

'Am I sure? Gawd! What stone did you crawl out from?'

'Okay, who else?'

'Ian Dury.'

'I've heard of him.'

'And so you should have. *Wake up and Make Love To Me.* Ooh!' Colette gave a little screech. '*Rise on this occasion half way up your back, sliding down your body, touching your behind.* Would you like if I did it to you?'

'Don't be stupid,' I said. Her hands were on my knees. I loved the feeling. But I was afraid Colm would come back. Or the other girls would notice.

One of the leaving certs supervised the clearing away of desks and all the first-years rushed to the record player. Colette stood squinting at them. 'That one with the red hair has nice legs. Betchya anything she'll put on Gilbert O'Sullivan.'

The red-haired first-year was holding the needle, wincing as she concentrated on putting it at the right part of the vinyl. Someone jogged her elbow, and she stuck her tongue out in frustration.

'She shouldn't have bothered being so careful,' Colette said.

The song shot on half way into the first verse and Gilbert O'Sullivan was singing '*You're a bad dog, baby.*' God, that song was so old. It would have been laughed out of my old school. The first-years did a special dance. Really stupid. Heeling the ground twice and then changing sides with their partner and repeating the movement until the record ended. They were really into the heeling. It made them look like ponies at the circus. They had fierce important looks on their faces.

'*You're a bad dog, baby,*' they shouted. Louder than Gilbert O'Sullivan who got drowned out.

Trish came over to where we were standing, 'Colm is back,' she said dejectedly.

Colette pulled the elastic band off Trish's ponytail and Trish's hair fell down to her shoulders. That was one thing about Trish. She had nice hair. It wasn't light or bright like Colette's, but it was fierce symmetrical. Three straight black sheets that lay down obediently. And it wasn't that she was a tidy person otherwise. Her uniform was always crumpled, her socks hanging down. Her nails had black under them half the time.

'Is your hair just naturally so tidy?' I asked, putting my hand out and touching her hair. Trying to work out the secret.

'It's awful, isn't it? Dead straight. My mother used to torture me with curlers when I was small, but she could never get a curl.' Trish began to twirl a strand around her finger.

'Don't let Colm see you,' Colette said and added in

Colm's voice, 'Take your hand down from your hair. Rid yourself of that awful habit. It's a very bad sign of character. The sign of a shifty person. Like a man who won't meet your eyes.'

Colette moved across the floor, lifting her hands and legs in the air as she went, pretending to be a puppet.

'God, I hope she's okay,' I said in a low voice to Trish.

'Colette?' Trish laughed. 'Don't worry about her. She'll be fine. Don't worry about her,' she said it again, as if she was telling herself as well.

'What's her brother like?'

'Johnny?'

'Yes.'

'He's a quietish sort of fellow.'

'*Quiet?*'

The record stopped, and a Strauss waltz came on. The first-years were shouting and raging. Colette made her way over to Trish and me, telling the first-years: 'You can't have everything your own way. I've put this on for the fifth-years. It's more cultured.'

The first-years muttered 'lousy' a few times and then began to dance again. They heeled slowly and lightly this time and were much quieter as they didn't have to join in at the chorus.

'I had to rescue you,' Colette said, as we swirled around the floor waltzing to the *Blue Danube.*

'I didn't need rescuing,' I said, half annoyed with her for being so possessive.

'You don't know Trish as well as I do,' Colette's eyes became slitty and knowing. 'She's not as straightforward as she seems.'

'How do you mean?'

'Well, for starters, she's got a violent temper.'

'Trish?'

'I'm only telling you. Take it or leave it,' Colette said

and her hand tightened around my waist and then moved up my back. It was kind of pleasant and I shivered.

'You're cold,' said Colette and pulled me closer as if she had been waiting for her chance. I let her pull me right up against her body. She was very warm.

'*Do, do, do, do, do, DO, DO, do, do,*' Colette hummed and then charged around the study, holding me very close against her. 'Are you going to come to my bed tonight?' she whispered, her cold lips against my ear.

'What if we get caught?'

There was a sharp scraping noise from the top of the study, and Mother Colm began making her way down from her chair. Colette danced even more slowly. Mother Colm stopped in front of our entwined bodies. She walked round us and surveyed us from different angles. Colette kept singing, I thought I'd die with mortification, but I couldn't bring myself to break away. Besides, Colette was holding me really tight and she was fierce strong. Away stronger than I was.

'Can you not keep your hands off that girl?' Colm wheezed.

I felt really hot.

'No, Sister, I can't,' Colette said and kept on dancing.

Mother Colm gave me a vicious look. It was really unfair the way she always seemed to be crosser with me. Why did the nuns say nothing to Colette? Was it because she was never caught actually doing anything wrong? It annoyed me and I broke away from Colette, pushing hard on her arms. I sat down next to Trish. Trish was doing a crossword. I tried to help, but Colette insisted on humming the *Blue Danube* loudly beside us. And bouncing a tennis ball against the wall.

'Put that ball down this instant! You'll have the

wall ruined, Colette MacSweeney.' Mother Colm shouted, looking at me indignantly.

'Right oh, Sister,' Colette put the ball down and when Mother Colm walked away toward the study door, added, 'She's only annoyed because we're keeping her away from sweet Noreen. If she didn't have to be looking after us, they could be talking in Irish to their hearts' content.'

The study door slammed as Mother Colm left and the stained-glass panels shivered. I thought that the glass would shatter.

'And good riddance!' called Colette after the closing door. 'Go 'way and say some rosaries for yourself.'

She took up the tennis ball again and threw it really hard against the wall. Just over the heads of a few first-years. They looked kind of pleased that she picked their section of the wall. As if they were living dangerously. The study door opened again and Mother Colm returned with Sister Paul, who looked even bigger with importance. Her two grey eyes were joined up.

'Stop that! Break it up! Break it up!' Sister Paul moved in on a few first-years who were waltzing cheek to cheek. 'We can't have that!' she said with a light-hearted laugh to show that all was well. 'Whoever could have been teaching you to dance like that?' She looked fiercely at me, while Mother Colm nodded ominously beside her.

'I'm here to show a good example,' Sister Paul insisted, and with one dramatic movement lifted the arm of the record player. 'Now we'll have some nice Irish music,' she said and played an awful creaky old-fashioned march on the record player. 'Separate yourselves, separate yourselves. It's the golden rule for ladies,' she ordered the first-years. She began to march, swinging her arms. 'Everybody must join in. Come on, now.' She glared at us.

Trish and I got to our feet and Colette followed our lead, smiling sarcastically, hissing, 'Stoopid,' in an underground voice. Sister Paul led us all round the study in a bottle-green snake, our slippered feet padding on the old, polished, green, brown and white tiles.

Colette had taken her jumper off and the golden skin at the opening of her blouse had turned pink. She winked at me and squeezed my elbow. I gave a quick look at Sister Paul, but she was looking ahead proudly.

'O'Neill's march into battle,' she raised her hoarse voice. 'And never forget you're all little soldiers. Little soldiers of the Convent of the Sacred Heart.' She flung open the study door and led us down the corridor.

'Sharp left,' she said and we all turned, past the bell rope with its knitted green cover and up the brass staircase. Up and up, we climbed as O'Neill's march faded. The staircase was made of polished golden wood, with a brass plate on every step where you put your foot. Colette sneaked her arm around my waist. The line of marching girls thickened and became untidy as we waited at the top for more instructions.

Paul stopped, her large white face had turned red and sweaty. She tried to smile benevolently at the first-years, but it came out like an ugly grin. 'Keep your hands to yourself and learn to stand up on your own two feet.'

She climbed away up the steps to her attic bedroom, without even a 'goodnight'.

Everybody delayed before making their way to their dormitories. The first-years had to go back down the stairs again as their dormitories were on the middle corridor. The leaving certs waited until they could hear the sound of Sister Paul's bedroom door closing, before clumping up to their own rooms in the attic dormitory.

Colette linked her arm with mine as we slowly walked into Saint Joseph's dormitory. The room smelt of soap and talc, mixed with the close odour of hair and shampoo. We pulled the curtains and lay down together on my bed. Colette stroked my neck and the inside of my arms, and we listened to the rushing sounds of everyone else getting ready for bed.

· Six ·

Saturday morning, we didn't have to go to Mass. Saturday morning was for changing sheets and washing hair. We were supposed to dust our lockers and clean under the bed. Then we had to take our sheets to the laundry.

I hadn't any clean shirts left. Except for one and I had to keep that clean for Sunday. So I put my pinafore on over the top of my pyjamas. 'It looks like a blouse anyway,' I told myself, knotting my tie in front of the mirror. Colette said she would wash my hair and dry it upside down. She said it was going to look *brill.*

Making my bed quickly and swishing a tissue quickly over the dust on my locker, I looked around for Colette. She wasn't in her bed. Trish said she thought that Colette had gone for breakfast and we went down to the refectory to see. She wasn't there either. I wanted to go and look for her again, but Trish made me sit down and have a bowl of cornflakes with her.

'There's no need to worry about Colette. She's fine. Probably gone to have a fag somewhere.'

I thought that I'd better look unconcerned and said, 'Who? Oh Colette!' as if I'd forgotten all about her. 'Mmm. Well.' And stared out the window at the tennis courts. But I was fierce disappointed. I had been looking forward to getting my hair done.

'Haven't you washed your hair yet?' Trish asked. 'All the hot water will be gone.'

'Oh, I always wash it with cold. It's very good for the head.'

'How's that?' Trish asked. I could see damp limp cornflakes on the tip of her tongue as she spoke.

I looked away. 'It closes the pores.'

There was no one left in the blue bathroom. I picked the biggest bath and filled my jug. It was cold. Taking a deep breath I poured it over my head. And after the first shock and the pain that spread, my head went slowly numb. I rubbed the shampoo into my cold blocky head. It felt heavy. As if it didn't belong to me. I pressed my hand hard against my temples, thinking that I could be brain-damaged.

After wrapping my orange towel around my head, I staggered into the dormitory like a man who had been shot. I felt dizzy and weird, as I made my unsteady way to the bed.

'You're like the Shah of Persia!' Colette said as she revved her hair dryer in the corner of the dormitory. She was wearing her A-line bottle-green Sunday uniform and a see-through white blouse. Her blonde hair fell into her eyes, sliding and falling. All over the place.

'Were you smoking?'

'None of your business, Mother Superior.'

'I was just asking.'

'And I'm just telling you.'

'Okay, fine, fine,' I said and sat down to try and rub some feeling back into my scalp.

'Well, if you must know,' Colette said. 'I was ringing home.'

'And were they okay?' I asked sympathetically.

'Of course they were!' Colette pushed her hair back

off her forehead and stood up very straight. Looking wild and free. At the fireplace. 'Johnny has got a new motorbike. It sounds brilliant. Oh, I wish it was mid-term break. I can't wait to see it!'

I felt awful, because I could wait for the mid-term break. I could wait to see my mother. And I hated the thought of not being with Colette. Colette looked at me for a moment. To make sure I was really jealous. But before I became demented, 'Come down by the window and I'll do your hair.' Colette held my hand and squeezed it lightly. She unplugged the dryer and we moved the combs and brushes down to the windowsill.

Colette sniffed, 'Your hair smells brilliant. What is it?'

'Cold water and Sunsilk,' I said, feeling sorry for myself.

'You should try Milk Plus Six. It's fucking fantastic.' Colette dried my hair upside down for a few minutes. She was really ferocious about it, running her fingers through my scalp as she moved the drier in and out. And every now and then blowing hot and cold alternate draughts down my neck. Making me jump and squeal. And feel silly. When she was finished, she lifted my head up and hair fell dry and soft all over my face.

'What's it like?' I asked.

'Wild, man. It's wild, man,' she said, combing it lightly. She spent ages threading the comb through the hairs and raising tremors over my scalp. Sometimes she lifted the comb up high and let my hair fall from the comb. It fanned its way down slowly. Colette said it was full of electricity.

'I always wanted a go at long hair,' she said, and I was glad that my hair was long. The sun shining through the glass toasted my skin. I felt sleepy. Colette ran the comb through my hair so lightly, it hardly seemed real. I leaned against her and closed my eyes.

I jumped like mad when I heard Colm's voice. Loud and horrible, 'Will you leave that girl's hair alone, Colette MacSweeney! And you, Grace Jones, take that mopish look off your face. You look like someone who's had electric shock treatment.' Mother Colm rocked back and forth on her black heels, getting the most out of her outrage.

'Yes, Mother Colm,' said Colette mockingly, picking up the comb and the brush and the two mirrors she'd been using to show me the back of my hair. She blatantly imitated Colm, waddling her behind and sticking her jaw out as she went back to her cubicle.

I went to follow her, but Mother Colm caught my arm. 'What is that you're wearing under your uniform?'

'It's a blouse, Mother.'

'It looks to me very like the top of a pyjamas!'

'I'll take it off,' I said. Wishing that she would go away.

'Well, I don't know where your mother got you! She's the most elegant woman I've ever seen and you, you're like a tramp.'

'Sorry, Mother.'

'I don't think you're sorry at all,' Mother Colm stood back looking at me, folding her arms. 'Your poor mother that's all I can say!' she finished finally. 'Go away and get properly dressed.'

After breakfast, study started at ten o'clock. Some of the leaving certs straggled in late, their hair still wet. They made the study look dreary, with their wet flattened serpent-like heads, bent over their books.

At twelve o'clock I went to confessions with Colette. Everybody went. Every Saturday. They were either religious or wanted to get into shops. It was the only time we got to go to town and we weren't supposed to go into shops. They sent two nuns with us to make sure.

You tried to keep away from the nuns, but sometimes you got stuck with them. That's what happened to Colette and me. We bumped into Mother Colm and old Sister Benedicta at the door of the cloister. Colette stooped to tie her shoelace to let them go ahead. It looked desperate obvious. 'Well I have to do something,' she said and stuck up her two fingers behind their backs.

Benedicta clung tightly to Colm's arm. She was half blind which was a good thing. We walked slower and slower to let them go ahead. It was hard, because Benedicta was a really useless walker.

We caught sight of the sea every now and then between the bungalows that lined the road into town. It was grey and flat, yet wide and free-looking. And it could have been nice if it wasn't for the dirty salmon-pink garage stuck in the middle of it.

'Pity about the garage,' I said.

'Don't mind the view,' Colette pulled me on. 'We've got to get to Smarts before the nuns get hold of us.'

Smarts was in the square, it was a fantastic sweet shop. We stopped for a moment outside the window to look at the coloured jars. Pineapple Chunks, Rum and Butters, Malt and Creams, Scots Clan, Emerald, Choffees, Pear Drops, they had everything. Broken chocolate and Scrumble bars were sold cheap. I couldn't wait to get in and we were just pulling the glass door open, when Sister Benedicta and Mother Colm suddenly came back. We couldn't believe it when we saw the two black heaps of clothing moving towards us again.

'Fuck, fuck, fuck,' Colette hissed under her breath and pulled me towards the shop window next door. We stood and stared at some thick grey knitted men's socks and wellington boots. I thought we looked really fishy. The nuns came and stood next to us and looked as well. Mother Colm gave smug looks out of the corner of her eye. She knew we were thwarted.

'Are you interested in wellingtons?' Sister Benedicta asked us.

'Very,' Colette said.

'Fishing is a grand hobby.' Benedicta squinted at a pair of kingfisher-blue short wellies. Her eyes were watering.

'And, wasn't Christ himself a fisherman?' I said, trying to be nice. But half ashamed in front of Colette. Colette's eyes went really slitty and Mother Colm gave me a suspicious look. Sister Benedicta's mouth was round with admiration. 'Well, aren't you the wise little one!' she beamed. 'Oh the innocent face of her,' she said to the sky and started to grope under her skirts.

I looked away while she lifted loads of black layers and found a pocket in a wide pair of black bloomers. She took out a plastic box and inside was a pale pink rosary on a bed of cotton wool. I stood there, feeling really stupid, knowing I was going to get the beads and not wanting them.

Benedicta held them out with sacred hands. I was fierce embarrassed.

'Aren't they beautiful?' Colette said and impatiently shoved them into my hand. 'We must fly or we'll be late for confessions, Sister.'

'Oh the little angels,' Sister Benedicta said to Mother Colm, gazing blindly at us, her blue eyes streamy with cataracts.

Colette dragged me off and, as we ran to the parish church she shouted into the wind, 'God almighty! We would get stuck with that edjit while everyone else was getting away with murder. I wanted to go to the Emmet grill for chips.'

'What about your diet?'

'Jesus, I have to have some reward. I can't be suffering all the time.'

The old parish church smelled damp, and small altars, heavy with candles, made bright caves in the dark. I went to Saint Anthony's altar and took out two candles. I loved the waxy feel of them and the heat of all the other candles on my face when I leaned in to put my candles in the holders. I looked in my purse, but I only had a pound. I wasn't going to put a whole pound in. I'd have to pay it back some other time. I kind of half-promised, because I kind of half-believed. I felt guilty about the candles, because I'd been doing it for years. Lighting them and not paying. Even when I was religious.

'Get up! Get up!' Colette shook my arm. 'Colm and Ben are in. We've got to go.'

'I want to light one more. Look, the one in the right hand corner has just gone out.' I felt superstitious about it.

'Too late, too late. We must go now.'

'What about confessions?'

'Surely you don't think we came here for confessions?'

Colette dragged me down the aisle towards the enormous wooden doors.

'Well,' I hesitated in the porch to dip my fingers in the holy water stoup. 'You'd like to be on the safe side.'

'Safe side! Telling your sins to those perverts. Do you think that I came down to tell Father Hognett about every time I have a wank? You must be joking! I come down town to buy sweets and chips!'

We ran all the way to Smarts. I felt like beating the woman behind the counter, she was so slow. I kept thinking that Colm was behind us. I rushed my choices and ended up feeling sorry that I hadn't got Malt and Creams instead of Rum and Butters.

We walked back to the school, but this time I didn't notice the grey sea between the bungalows or the ugly salmon-pink garage. I thought about my stolen candles burning brazenly in the parish church. Some day it would catch up with me. And I was wondering what in the hell was a wank.

· Seven ·

I was sitting on Colette's bed, swinging my legs. Trish sat on the floor. I was getting a bit sick of Trish, she was either in a bad mood, telling us to 'Cop on,' or she was like she was tonight, friendly and determined to stay in the way. Colette was doing loads of exercises. She had done one hundred sit ups, fifty leg stretches on each side and now she was going to beat her previous record of two hundred waist twists.

It wore me out, looking at her. I lay down on the bed and watched her face, contorting and grimacing. It was all pink and shiny. And still she looked nice. She wore a long T-shirt that came just to the top of her long legs. I thought she looked brilliant.

'Sing to me,' she said, every now and then, and I laughed.

Of course I wasn't going to sing. It was only someone like Colette that could sing out of tune and still sound okay. Make the song even better. That was because she really did have a good voice. But it was weak and she mocked it. And then the weakness sounded the best part of it.

'You sing,' I said.

'Okay, wait a minute!' Colette began to twist her

waist faster and more savagely. 'Just give me a minute,' and she hacked her body each way. 'I must be thin for Christmas.'

Her face got redder and redder and her cheeks bulged. And just when she was beginning to look really awful, she stopped. It took her a few minutes to get her breath back.

'You're going to give yourself a heart condition.' Trish was talking like she was fifty.

'Not I,' Colette gasped and she wasn't able to say any more for a few minutes. Just stood there, wiping her face and chest and arms with yellow tissues, and panting.

'Actually, I think I'll have a wash!' she said and gave a grin to Trish. She pulled off her T-shirt. She had nothing on except a small pair of purple knickers. They were about the same colour purple as her hands. I found it embarrassing. I wasn't a great one for naked bodies. There had been one glass shower at my last school and I never went near it.

'You're such an exhibitionist,' Trish said and frowned. 'You're like a skeleton.'

Colette pulled her breath in really tight and showed off her rib cage. I thought that she was perfect, but I didn't like her standing in front of us, half naked. I felt awful uncomfortable. Mainly because I was afraid that she would expect me to do the same. The way some people weigh themselves in front of you and then ask you to get on the scales. I really hated that. My cousin Delia was always doing it.

Colette soaped and soaped, making a lather all over her arms and chest. Showing off. I couldn't stick it another minute. 'Oh God, this is *so* boring. I must get back to my book.'

Colette caught her T-shirt, pulled it over her soapy body and threw herself down next to me. Holding my eyes in hers, she swished back her silky hair. 'But don't you find it so sexciting?'

I found it silly. But I liked it too. I never knew what I would do if we were alone. Sometimes I wished I were a different person. Someone who could throw herself into things. Or even throw my clothes off the way Colette did.

'Stop embarrassing Grace,' Trish said and I hated her.

'I'm not embarrassed,' I said.

'Of course she's not. She loves me,' Colette howled the word love like a wolf and pulled my head against her damp sleeve for a second.

'You never told us the story of *Deirdre of the Sorrows.*' Trish's latest thing was that we should do educational things with each other.

Colette sat up enthusiastically, 'Go on, why don't you tell it?'

'Are you sure you never heard it?' I said, not wanting them to say half way through the telling, 'Oh but we know that old thing,' the way people did when I told jokes sometimes.

'No we don't,' Colette said. 'We're positive.'

'Well,' I began, 'there was this beautiful young girl called Deirdre.'

'Like you,' Colette interjected and then said, 'I'm only joking.'

'Are you sure you want to hear this?'

'Sure we're sure,' Colette said, stroking my arm encouragingly.

'Well there was this girl, Deirdre, and the story is basically about her. Her story was full of sorrow.'

'Definitely like you,' Colette said, playing an imaginary violin.

'Oh for God's sake,' I said, fuming and folding my arms.

'Oh for God's sake, oh for God's sake,' Colette sang to the tune of the *Banana Splits* song, 'la la la, la la la, la la la, la la la la.'

I sulked and refused to continue. Then they became persuasive.

'You have to tell it now. You have to! The suspense is killing me.' Colette pretended to be really dramatic.

'You're really good at telling stories, come on,' Trish said and I found it hard not to give in.

'Oh, all right so,' I said, as if it was a big favour. 'But if there's one more interruption, I'm stopping. She was very sad because she was betrotted to the King of Ulster who was very rich, but desperate old.'

'What's betrotted?' Trish asked.

'It's the old word for being engaged,' I said, impatiently.

'You mean betrothed,' Colette corrected me. 'Where did you get betrotted, you old fool.' She began to giggle.

I went red. 'Stop interrupting. The king's name was Conchubhar and he knew she didn't want him, so he kept her in a house in the woods until they were ready to get married. And he'd come to visit her, and tell her that he was going to get her, and she'd say no, she wanted a young man with the hair of a raven and skin of snow and lips as red as if blood had been spilt on them.'

'God, she sounds like a right animal,' Colette said.

'It's a bit much all right, but that's the way they were then and it had to sound poetic. Anyway one night, three young men arrived, it was Naoise and the sons of Usna.'

'Hohoo,' Colette said, 'we're getting to the sexciting part.'

'It was love and was beautiful and so sad, because it was all foretold in the prophesy that the king got. But he paid no heed to it. Deirdre was even embroidering a tapestry of three huntsmen before she ever saw them. They arrived looking for shelter one day, and Naoise fell in love with Deirdre.'

'He'd no choice,' Colette interrupted.

'Why? Because she was beautiful?'

'No, because of the prophecy.'

'That's true, actually. It was like Jesus, he never had a chance either, he had to fulfil the scriptures. If he had tried to get out of it, everyone would have said he was a terrible coward.'

'Jesus, don't get religious, for God's sake.' Colette gave me a light belt across the shoulder.

'Well, you better stop interrupting me then,' I said, getting annoyed.

'Get on with the story,' said Trish.

'Oh yes, and they ran away, Deirdre and the sons of Usna. Deirdre's maid stayed behind and faced the music. Conchubhar went mad, he sent armies after them, they spent years fleeing from country to country. And do you know what he did that was really lousy?'

'No, but I'm all ears,' Colette said, screwing up her face.

I looked at her and then I did something weird. I kissed her. Not an ordinary kiss, but a kiss where our lips were exactly over each other's. And it felt nice. Kind of soft and warm, with lots of nerves beating. I felt stupid in front of Trish, though.

'Go on with the story, honeybunch,' Colette said.

'The really lousy part was,' I could hear my voice shake, 'Conchubhar would tell all the other kings in the other countries how beautiful Deirdre was and then they'd want to get her, chasing Deirdre and the sons of Usna all over the place. In the end, they were getting exhausted from all the fleeing, and Conchubhar promised to pardon them if they came back.' I stopped for a moment, dying for breath. 'But Deirdre didn't believe him. She kept saying that it was prophesied that they would be killed by the king. Naoise wanted to chance it anyway, even though Conchubhar was being very fishy. Conchubhar kept wanting to know if Deirdre had lost her beauty, with all the years' travelling. They came back even though Deirdre was dead against it and Conchubhar sent Deirdre's old maid to see if Deirdre was still beautiful and the maid went back and pretended that she had lost all her beauty and had gone all wrinkled. Conchubhar didn't believe her. He found out that Deirdre was still beautiful and he got the sons of Usna killed. Deirdre was heartbroken and stabbed herself and threw herself into the grave after them, rather than let Conchubhar get her.'

'Well she sounds a right fool, she could have married the king afterwards and have had Naoise as well and all the money,' Colette said.

'But she couldn't stand Conchubhar.' I was disappointed at the reception my story got. 'I think it's great. It was romantic. They were in love.'

'And I'm in love with you, and you keep rejecting me.'

'I don't!'

'Prove it,' Colette said, pulling me down in the bed on top of her chest.

I wanted to stay like that. But I couldn't because Trish was there. 'Don't be stupid!' I said, breaking away. Heaving myself over the side of the bed. Feeling really breathless.

'I must get back to bed,' I said.

'So must I,' Trish said, getting up heavily at last. I hated her again.

'Goodnight, Colette,' we called, but there was no answer.

· *Eight* ·

Auntie Catherine and my cousin, Delia, were staying with us for the weekend of the mid-term break. Though I liked Delia, I hated when they were there. When we were on our own together, my mother and I got on fine, she was loving towards me. But when Delia was around, she seemed to realise how inferior I was.

'You're getting fat,' my mother said.

'Ah, she's not, it's just her natural shape,' Delia said. Being nice as usual.

'Rounded,' said Auntie Catherine. I hated her.

I hated them all. Sitting like a fool, stuffed into a dress that was too tight. Supposed to be out for dinner. To eat. And enjoy myself. And they were talking about my weight. All because I said I'd have chips on the side. Delia was having melon for starters. I wanted vol-au-vents.

'That pastry!' my mother said. 'Why don't you take Delia's example and have melon? Look at her beautiful skin.'

Delia had a clear complexion and shiny hair. Delia was like an ad for young-looking skin. I couldn't help admiring her, and she was fierce brainy as well, studying electrical engineering at university. It impressed my mother no end, especially as she hadn't a clue about science. She thought it was mysterious. I wanted to be like Delia, studying something difficult. Mysterious myself.

I was missing Colette like mad. I imagined her on the motorbike with Johnny. I wondered what he was like. He was bound to be handsome. Trish said that he was like Colette.

My mother looked really nice. She had a bluey-green dress on. She had made it herself, but it didn't look it. And pearls on her neck. And her bun really high on top of her head. She left Auntie Catherine for dead. Auntie Catherine was kind of red and breathless looking. She didn't look like the one with the money.

Auntie Catherine was nice and she never said anything sharp or hurtful. On the other hand, she never said anything uplifting, the way Delia did sometimes when she was being nice. Still, I could have liked her more if she hadn't been so keen on Delia too. Of course she was Delia's mother, I understood that. But I wouldn't have minded someone thinking I was a bit special, seeing as my mother didn't. Delia was being really helpful, although sometimes I couldn't help noticing that she made most of her offers to help in front of my mother and didn't follow them up. I felt bad for noticing it, especially as I was sure that Delia didn't realise that she was doing it.

'Would you like a hand with your honours maths?' Right in front of the other two!

'Ah, no I'm fine,' I said.

'Grace!' my mother said in a warning voice.

'Thanks all the same.'

'God, you're great,' Delia said. 'I was completely muddled for the whole of the fifth year. It was only at the end, that they started coming to me.'

'It's not that I find them easy. I'm going to give them up.'

'Grace,' said my mother and her bun was expanding with the shock.

It was the cause of a terrible row. I didn't speak to my mother for the whole weekend. She didn't even know the first thing about honours maths or what I was good at. She just thought it sounded like something I should be doing. Not that she could add two and two herself.

We mediated through Delia, who was being fierce nice and supportive towards me when my mother wasn't around. And the funny thing was that she didn't seem to give one damn what I did.

'Well if you find it too hard, there's no point.' Delia shrugged her shoulders. She seemed to think that it was better that I didn't strain myself. So why the bloody hell did she have to bring it up in the first place?

I didn't want to say goodbye when they were going, but Delia came to look for me. She looked awful hurt.

'Grace, you're like my sister. You mean the world to me.' She held me against her chest. I got a rush of sisterly feeling towards her and felt bad about the trouble I'd caused all weekend. Delia looked deep into my eyes, flashing her clear healthy eyeballs at me. I felt bloodshot.

And then I started thinking about Colette. About how she touched me and everything. I pulled away from Delia. 'I'll come down to the car with you.'

'Oh, would you?'

It was fine then. I stood at the front waving with my mother. It was Sunday. Only a few hours and I'd be back with Colette.

My mother put her hand on my shoulder. 'It's okay,' she said. 'I'm sorry for putting pressure on you. Delia explained that you're not able for the honours maths.'

*

I thought we'd never get to Mayo. The road was forever. It seemed a year since we left home and a century since I'd seen Colette. Auntie Catherine had given me a fiver. I had a little fantasy about Auntie Catherine really preferring me. And having to cloak it in case she hurt Delia's feelings. In the small towns the street lights were yellow and when I half closed my eyes they went blurry with orange around the edges.

My mother spoke about Delia. 'She thinks the world of you, you know.'

'Does she?'

'Oh yes, she turned to me before she went and said that she often cries when she thinks about you.'

'Cries with frustration, I suppose.'

'Don't be always mocking, Grace, it doesn't suit you.'

'Well, I got it from you.'

'Grace, we're approaching the convent now. Are you going to say goodbye to me like this?'

'All right, all right. I'm sorry. I'm sorry. And I know Delia is really nice.'

'I'm glad you admit it. You're lucky to have her.' She indicated right as she swept up the convent avenue, the car roaring in second gear.

'Now, haven't we made good time,' she said and scraped along the statue of Angel Gabriel.

I met Trish at the cloister door.

'Have you heard?'

'No!' I was afraid that something had happened to Colette.

'Have you heard the news? Miss Pole is putting on a play and you've got the lead part already.'

'Without an audition?'

Trish nodded.

I was so excited I brought Trish back to the car to meet my mother.

'Hello, Mrs Jones.' Trish held out her hand.

'Hello.' My mother was cool, she was looking at Trish's dirty socks.

'Trish said that I'm going to have the lead part in a play and I haven't even been auditioned.'

'Stand up straight, Grace.' My mother patted her bun. 'Your posture is a disgrace. I'm surprised the nuns haven't said something to you.'

She was dying to get away. 'I haven't time to visit the Sisters, you must send them my regards.' My mother told Trish that it was lovely meeting her. In a bored and distant voice. Then she caught sight of Trish's protruding stomach. She gave it a worried look and then looked back at mine. As if she was afraid that I might catch it.

'Let her worry,' I thought and then felt half a pang watching her drive off. The country roads were dark and narrow and she was a useless driver. She backed out, hacking at the gears. Skimmed past the Angel Gabriel and roared away in second gear.

Colette was in bed when we arrived in Saint Joseph's dormitory. Combing her fair hair into her eyes. 'You're acting the part of Archibald and I'm going to be the French maid.'

'Are you in it as well?'

'Sure am!' Colette pushed the hair out of her eyes with a wild shake of her head.

'Who is Archibald?'

'He's the main character, but he's really a girl dressed up as a boy. It's all about these girls in an English boarding school and one of them needs a date, so one of the other girls dresses up as a boy and that's you, Archibald.'

'But that doesn't sound like me.'

'Miss Pole thinks it is. I'm a French maid for God's sake!'

'Did you have a good weekend?' Trish asked me.

'It was brilliant,' I said.

'Mine was fab!' Colette said. I was disappointed she didn't say more. I thought she'd talk about Johnny and the new bike, but I was too jealous to ask. Maybe I'd ask Trish later. They came from the same village. That's why Colette's parents sent her to Mayo. They wanted Trish to keep an eye on her. I thought that was hard on Trish. It wasn't as if she could stop Colette from doing anything.

Then Colette said the most horrible thing.

'You're getting fat, especially around the bottom.'

'I'm not,' I said, mortified. During this weekend, I had had to open the button of my Levis every time I sat down.

'You are so. You'd make two of Trish and she's bad.'

'Your mother is very young-looking,' said Trish. I knew she was trying to be nice.

'Which is more than you are,' Colette continued. 'Honestly, you look about twenty-six, the way you're going around with those hunched up shoulders.'

I flicked back my hair. Trying not to show that there were tears in my eyes.

'But don't worry, I love you just the way you are.' Colette put her purple hand on mine.

'And I'm not staying here to be insulted.' I flounced off, feeling really stupid. I pulled my curtains and lay on the bed. I was a heaving mountain. I was fat and blotchy. I was crying and everything. I hated everyone. Auntie Catherine, my mother, Delia. But especially Colette.

· *Nine* ·

I had loads of lines to learn. Twice a week, we left study for rehearsals. All the other girls stared when we went out. You couldn't help feeling important. Mother Colm looked savage. She tried to ignore us, but Colette always went up to ask for permission to leave. Mother Colm used to nod vaguely, and pretend to be engrossed in something crucial. Threading a needle or drawing a margin.

Colette wouldn't let her get away with it though. 'Thank you, Mother. Thank you, Mother.' And even the swots would look up. Colette was so loud.

Trish was playing the part of two schoolgirls called Zenobia and Boadicea. She had to change three times during the play. When she was playing the part of Zenobia, she had just one line to say. 'Oh gosh, be a boy and wear those horrid tweedy things.' Boadicea said nothing.

The school hall was always warm, not like the study. It was new and it smelt of wood. Our stockinged feet made pounding hollow noises as we moved around the stage. Everybody admired Miss Pole's figure as she needled between the actors, fixing our hand movements. Sometimes she put her leg on a chair, while she thought about a problem on the stage. She wore huge brown bell-bottom trousers. They draped and swung and hung on her slim body as she walked around, thinking. Sometimes she leaned the point of her elbow on her knee. Everyone stared at her while she concentrated. Sometimes she looked at us blankly as if she was wondering at what we were doing there. Or what she was doing there.

When the others were rehearsing, I squeezed together with Colette on the bottom rung of a step ladder that stood in front of the stage. Once I lost my balance and swayed backwards. Colette caught me just as I almost toppled off the stage. Colette hugged me for ages afterwards. 'What would I do if you were dead?' Miss Pole gave us a weird look.

My music lessons became a real pain. I wasn't practising. I was still doing the same tune after three months. A waltz called *Wonderland.* Sister Marie Therese sat belching and complaining beside me, waving a wooden stick. She rapped my knuckles every time I made a mistake. She was really ancient, and she wore the old-fashioned veil. It looked like a box with a cloth thrown over it, like something you'd see on the altar. It squeezed her old skin. You could see where it pinched her under the chin. She couldn't stop burping and sometimes she got the hiccups, but I had to play on. Or get a slap on the knuckles. I think it was all that trapped wind that made her cross. She had retired from music teaching, but had taken me on as a special favour because the other music nuns were fully booked.

Colette said that Marie Therese could drop dead at any moment. That made me afraid, as strange winds and substances gurgled and roared about the tubes of Marie Therese's digestive system. I hit the wrong keys and with the wrong timing. Marie Therese groaned and smacked my fingers with her wooden baton, 'Ah you're no good! Why won't you practise? You would have a grand touch on the keys if you weren't so nervous. You have the right fingers, all you need to do is practice.' She peered at my face and pushed at my hair with her stick. 'It's the way your hair is hanging into your eyes. Tie your hair in two horns the next time you come.'

I arrived with my hair in pigtails and Sister Marie Therese was really pleased. 'The horns suit you,' she said. I sat there feeling bald and conscious of the two devilish projections from my head. They cast shadows over the keys.

Colette gave me a loan of *The Exorcist.* I shouldn't have read it. I saw a small goblin devil crouching at the top of the curtains round my bed. Then I started getting strange smells and I didn't dare mention it to the others in case they were getting them as well. I was livid with fear every night, sniffing sulphur and imagining that green hands were scampering away under the bed when I approached. I was afraid that if I looked in the glass at night I would see the devil's face. If I had to get up to go to the toilet, I would shield my face as I passed the mirror.

I started getting earaches. I had to go to bed, and Sister Carmel brought me hot milk and Panadols. The earaches didn't improve and one of the nursing sisters came to see me. She said that it was probably an abscess and that I must see a doctor. Sister Carmel wrapped a big creamy yellow wool scarf around my head, she said the school scarf wasn't long enough, and I went off with Colette to see Doctor Buckley who lived on the outskirts of town.

It was a long walk and the long yellow scarf kept unwinding. Colette fixed it eventually by wrapping it around several times and then tying a big bow under my chin.

'You don't mind looking stupid?' she asked.

'I don't care, I don't care, anything for relief,' I moaned.

Along the Castle Road, where Doctor Buckley lived, there were lots of trees and shrubs, but in Doctor Buckley's garden everything was dead. An old woman let us in. The hall was dark and dusty. An old hallstand held stacks of black umbrellas. The woman led us to the surgery.

'Himself will be along in a minute.'

She looked like a woman who needed a cigarette to hang in the corner of her mouth.

It was really old-fashioned. And dusty. Strange metal instruments were laid out on a table covered in green cloth.

'He's going to torture you first. To make you talk,' Colette said in a threatening voice. She made me lie down on the old green leather couch and take off my shoes.

'It's only my ear!'

'Oh he's going to give you a full examination, you'll have to take everything off, girl.'

'I won't!' I was afraid that he would see how fat I was.

'Do you know what they say about Doctor Buckley?'

'No.'

'He likes young girls.'

The door opened and Doctor Buckley came in. I was sure that he must have heard Colette. It was really embarrassing. He was old and thin with silvery hair and his face had a purple tint.

'You're all ready for me, I see.' He gave a loud cough. I sat up, awkward and embarrassed.

'Now girleen, what's the problem?' He examined my

ear with a cold metal instrument that was like a flash-lamp. Then, he put it down and called the housekeeper. She came back with some batteries and he fitted them into the back of the instrument. He looked in again.

'A nasty bit of business, all right. We'll put you on some antibiotics. And what would you say to a bit of time off?'

'I don't know,' I said, sheepishly but hopefully.

'She's dying for it,' Colette said.

'I thought as much,' Doctor Buckley said and suddenly gave me a wet kiss on my forehead. Colette gave a big snort.

'Well I can't let ye two beautiful ladies go without offering you some tea.' He called the housekeeper and we all went down to kitchen. Mrs A. spread a white linen table cloth on the kitchen table. She put out some china cups and saucers. Doctor Buckley put me into an armchair by the range.

'I have to take special care of my patient,' he took a cardboard box tied with string out of the cupboard. 'I anticipated your call, Sister Carmel rang me and told me to take special care of you.'

We sat for about an hour eating doughnuts and drinking tea and chatting. Colette kept sniggering and making faces behind his back. I ignored her, genteely sipping my tea with my little finger stuck out, and making polite conversation. Then Dr Buckley said he had to make a phone call and went out.

Mrs A. took out a packet of Gold Flake. 'Do ye mind if I smoke?'

'Jesus, I thought you'd never ask, I'm dying for one,' Colette said putting out her purple hand.

I thought Mrs A. would be mad, but she was okay. 'Don't let him catch you. Do you want one?' she turned to me.

'No thanks.'

She shrugged her shoulders. I think she thought that I was casting judgement.

It was a strain waiting there while Colette blew gushes of smoke out her nose and Mrs A. looked at the clock.

'Sister Carmel wouldn't be too happy,' she said and jumped. 'There! He's just put the phone down. Give it here to me.' She fired it into the sink.

Dr Buckley threw open the door, looking excited. 'It's started to rain, so I've organised a lift for you with a handsome young gentleman.' We looked at each other. We couldn't arrive back to the convent with a handsome young gentleman.

'And what will the nuns say?' Mrs A. asked as she threw her wet half cigarette in the bin.

'I'll get him to drop you off at the bottom of the avenue.' Doctor Buckley moved his eyebrows up and down. I think it was supposed to be kind of appealing. Or cute or something. It looked stupid.

'Oh all right so, but we better not get caught,' Colette warned.

'Thanks very much,' I said. Colette kept making signs behind his back that he was mental. Mrs A. got a fit of laughing and left the room.

Doctor Buckley paced around the kitchen, jingling the coins in his pocket. 'Any minute now, your young gentleman will arrive.' His long skinny legs were going every way. His navy trousers reminded me of a postman.

Somebody blew a horn, and we went out to the front. The young gentleman was fat and greasy looking and he was humped over the wheel of an old Ford Cortina. Doctor Buckley asked us to say hello to Jerome. Jerome didn't speak or move. A flicker passed quickly across his face and he started up the car.

'Jerome, give the ladies a chance to get in,' Doctor Buckley appealed and said apologetically, 'Jerome is a bit of a tearaway but his heart is in the right place. I'm sure ye'll get on great.'

I tried to look cheerful as we got into the car. Colette muttered furiously, 'Would you just look at this for scutting! Gentleman my eye!'

I waved to Doctor Buckley.

'Take care of these young ladies, Jerome. Guard them with your life.'

Jerome grunted and the car shot off. We drove to the convent in silence as Jerome accelerated through town. Driving in the middle of the road and swerving violently around corners. I tried not to look at him, but my eyes were drawn back again and again to his round shoulders and the dark stains of sweat on his shirt. The stains seemed to be spreading every minute. He could have been sweating with shyness. I didn't want to think about it. He spoke only once. 'I thought ye were in a rush,' he smirked as we held tightly to the back of his seat.

Nobody saw us as we crept out of his rusty Cortina at the bottom of the convent avenue. Colette wouldn't even glance at him. I said goodbye, but I could not look at his face. I said it to his shoulder. He said nothing, just tore the gears and drove off.

Colette was boiling. 'I'll tell you one thing, if we get into trouble over that fat slob, I'll have Buckley in court.'

'For what?'

'Shut up!'

Colette tore up the avenue. And we got soaked anyway, because the avenue was so long.

· *Ten* ·

I was in bed for a few days and I spent the whole time reading *Gone With The Wind*. When Colette teased me, I said 'Fiddle dee dee' and tossed my head. Being an actress, I could do these things. And Colette would say, 'You're getting as fat as a fool.' She came up to the dormitory every day after school and we learnt our lines together. Trish wanted to come too but Colette told her she was banned.

'You've only got one line to say. If you don't know that at this stage, God help you. *We* are artistes, please don't disturb us.'

I was pleased now that we were alone, even though it was lousy on Trish, but I still wasn't comfortable with Colette. I liked watching her, she was so beautiful, but when she touched me I couldn't take it,

She stood in front of my mirror, practising her lines. Rolling her r's. Sounding French. She was good at it. That must have been why Miss Pole picked her. She tied her hair up high and put on the maid's lacy cap. She always wore it when she was rehearsing. Bits of fair hair came down at the sides. Because her hair was strained back, it made her eyes even slittier. And so greeny blue. The colour of Auntie Catherine's aquarium. Then she would slide onto the bed beside me and rub my arms. I liked that. Especially when she ran her fingers lightly along the crease of my elbow. Very relaxing. Until she started pulling me tightly on top of her body. And her breath coming faster. I couldn't take it. I wanted to, but I couldn't. I was always afraid one of the other girls would come in. Like the first-year, Brenda, with the pile of red hair. She came in once, looking for Trish, and stared at us, lying on the bed.

'We're trying to learn our lines, get out!' Colette said.

'Everyone else is learning theirs in the study.'

'Would you listen to this! Brazen as brass. *We* are artistes. Important people. She is an invalid,' Colette pointed to me. 'Now leave us.'

I was as nervous as a cat for ages after that.

I was still feeling weak the night we put on the play and as I waited in the wings, my head was fuzzy with fear. But when I started to say my lines, the fuzz became the roar of a lion and I strode around the stage purposefully. When I went out to the front of the stage to say, 'Is this the face that launched a thousand ships?' I stood right at the edge. Even the fear at the start had been enjoyable. Trish had rubbed my hands and Colette had rubbed my neck. I was the first to go on.

"We're all depending on you,' Colette said. And she was fierce funny. Her waist was so small in the little black maid's dress. All the first-years were talking about it. Even one of the leaving certs said something nice about her legs. I was glad because I had been afraid of being more successful than Colette.

Trish said afterwards that she was afraid that I would fall. But when I was on the stage, I knew I wouldn't fall, I was fearless and strong. The fact that I acted the part of a boy made me do masterful things. I put my leg up on a chair and spoke authoritatively. The best part was the feel of disguise and smell of the heavy stage make-up. Miss Pole had put on the make-up. It took ages. She was still patting and smudging long after the leaving certs had finished doing all the other faces. Colette was jealous.

'I saw you simpering when Miss Pole said your skin was so soft. Don't you know that she says that to everyone?'

'I didn't,' I said, feeling flattened.

'Oh, she'd say anything to get the best out of you. She was worried about only one thing.'

'And what's that?'

'To make sure the play was a big success.' Colette put her arm round me. 'But don't worry, I love you for yourself.'

Miss Pole brought Mikado and Kimberly biscuits for afterwards and Sister Carmel arrived with the orange squash.

'You were marvellous, Grace,' Sister Carmel squeezed my hand. 'And you too, Colette,' she was a bit slow bringing Colette into it.

Colette turned her back and said to me in a low voice, 'Call this a party. It's a bloody disgrace.'

'I think it's fine,' I said, 'and I don't like your attitude to Carmel.'

'All right, all right,' Colette bent forward and whispered in my ear. 'I've got something to tell you.'

'What?' I could smell the ginger biscuits on her breath.

'Colm is going to Stratford on Avon next weekend with the leaving certs. We'll have the dormitory to ourselves, at last!'

'But what about Trish?'

'Ah, that's the beauty of it! She's going home for her brother's ordination.'

It was exciting. I wondered how I'd manage. It was awful to want something and then not be able to take it when you got it. Colette kissed me quickly on the lips again. Her ginger breath was brilliant. She said, 'You know, I don't think Miss Pole is that thin, after all. She's got very funny bubbles on the insides of her thighs.'

· *Eleven* ·

Colette was tickling me and sticking her hand down the back of my Levis. They were loose again because I was beginning to find it easy not to eat. I couldn't stop laughing and wishing that Trish wasn't watching. I knew I was being stupid, but there was no way I could stop. We were so bad, Mrs Joyce shouted at us during elocution.

We were wearing our Levis because Mrs Joyce said she wanted us to do some simple limbering up exercises before she spoke about deportment. I wondered if she would make us walk around the room with books on our heads, the way my mother did with me. 'Here's my head, my bottom's coming,' my mother used to say in an attempt to shame me into walking properly.

'It has come to the Sisters' attention that some girls are not aware of the correct posture, and they have asked me to say a few words.'

Jesus. Now I would be made an example of, the way my mother always said I would. But Mrs Joyce went on to talk about crossing your ankles when you were sitting down. What she was really saying was don't sit with your legs wide apart. I relaxed then. I always sat with my ankles tightly crossed so Mrs Joyce wasn't talking to me.

Colette moved to the seat behind me, and plaited my hair. Little shivers ran up and down my back. Then a really strong shiver ran up my spine and I shuddered, shaking myself like a dog. Colette began to laugh and Mrs Joyce told us to leave.

'You leave me no choice,' she said, curling up her brown nose.

We felt ashamed only for a few minutes. We needed to get out anyway. I was full of dread and excitement. Mother Colm was on the bus for Holyhead. And so were all the leaving certs.

'It's *we* should be going to Stratford on Avon. We are the actresses. We are the artistes,' Colette said.

It was as if we were on holiday. We went along the walks. An old lay nun was working in the vegetable garden. The nuns that worked on the farm and in the garden were weird. They had so many shawls wrapped around them they had no shape. Once I saw one of them driving cows into a field. She had a stick. The hair stood up on the back of my neck. As if she was an apparition or something. We said hello to this nun and she smiled. She had only a few teeth. I thought that made her look even more mysterious. Like those women you'd see in photographs of evictions. In our history books. There was one other thing about these nuns. You just knew that they were really nice.

'She's got the face of a saint,' I whispered after we'd passed her out.

'And a great tan,' Colette said. To annoy me. When we got to Our Lady's grotto at the top of the walks, I sat on the kneeler in front of the altar, while Colette started doing her usual high kicks. She lifted her arms above her head and grasping one of the rafters in the roof of the shrine swung her whole body to and fro. I watched her and felt the whole evening slow down. Colette was wearing a red check shirt that had faded and had gone a bit pinkish. All the different reds had run into each other in the wash and it was very soft to touch. I wore a white embroidered cheesecloth top that my aunt had sent from New York. Colette said that I looked like a hippy, wearing that shirt, with my long hair down around my face. I was very flattered.

At twenty to seven, we crept back for the rosary. Mother Colm had left Noreen O'Donovan in charge. We refused to say the rosary, giggling and scuffling behind our chairs as Colette tried to put her hand up my jumper. Noreen O'Donovan said, 'You think you're so smart, Colette MacSweeney!'

Colette only laughed.

We were even worse in study after supper, when Noreen was supervising. Traipsing in and out the double glass doors. Refusing to stay quiet, sit down or do anything that she asked. Every time I looked at Noreen's small face, I heard Colm saying, 'If I had you now, I'd dress you always in cream and brown.' It really put me off.

'Noreen, you're going to have to let us go now,' Colette said, in a threatening voice. 'It's our bath night.' Noreen looked desperate relieved. Colette chased me up the brass staircase.

In the dormitory, we collected our bath things; flannels, soaps, bathsalts, bath towels. I picked up my orange bath towel and I began to quake inside. I wouldn't have been sorry to see Colm and the busload of leaving certs coming back.

In the blue bathroom, we filled our baths. Colette had bubble bath and we poured in loads of it. We had nearly a foot of bubbles. We got into our baths and Colette kept threatening to look over the wall. Somebody was in the last bath, but wouldn't answer when we called out. Colette said, 'Well, whoever you are, girl, you're splashing like an elephant.'

An awful silence answered Colette. The splashing stopped. I held my breath and then Colette tapped on my door. I got out quickly and wrapped the orange towel around me. Colette beckoned and I followed her to the window sill where she picked up a pink hot water bottle. I looked at it, my heart beating fast, pressing itself right out against my chest. The hot water bottle had 'Sister Mary Paul' written around its pink rubber neck.

We ran like mad and didn't stop until we got to my cubicle, breathless.

'Do you think it was Paul in the bathroom?' I gasped.

'It looks like it.'

'She's going to come after us, isn't she?'

'I don't know, why didn't she say something? I bet she was dodging prayers.'

I laughed. It could well be true. Paul seemed away more interested in exam results than holiness and she always rushed the Hail Mary before maths class. Paul would bully God in her prayers, 'Look, God this is what you have to do. Take heed, if you please and square your shoulders while I'm talking to you.'

Colette drew the yellow curtains around my bed and I reached into my locker for our stuff. Two cans of coke, a quarter pound of rum and raisin fudge, and a quarter pound of pear drops for dessert. Colette said that we could break our diets tonight. Probably bribing me.

We got into my bed and I pulled the covers right up. 'It's not cold,' Colette said, and threw back her side of the blankets. As we ate the fudge, I became more and more uncomfortable as the sound of chewing from my cheeks crashed against the inside walls of my ears. I stopped a few times to listen. You couldn't tell Paul that she was splashing like an elephant and expect to get away with it. Colette put her arm round me and I could feel myself stiffening. I shook myself and tried to loosen up. My teeth chattered.

'We better keep quiet until the lights are out, in case Paul comes to look for us,' I said, nervously.

'Scaredy cat!' teased Colette, squeezing me by the waist.

'I must wash my teeth!' I panicked as our big moment came near.

Then Colette got out of bed too and we both brushed our teeth at my wash basin. I began to feel hemmed in. I brushed my teeth for ages, white froth steaming on my lips. Colette lay back on my bed, looking luxurious, 'If you keep brushing your teeth like that, you'll knock them all out.'

By now, everybody else had come to bed and the sound of washing and scrubbing came from behind the yellow curtained cubicles.

'It's no harm to get rid of Trish for a while,' Colette said contentedly, her eyes fixed on my bare white legs.

'Don't look at my legs,' I said anxiously.

'Why not?'

'They're too fat.'

'No, they're fine. Your arse is a bit big all right, but your legs are okay. By Christmas you'll be grand. Are you doing those exercises I told you to do?'

The lights went out at that moment and I groped my way to the bed. Colette tried to kiss me and hold me against her chest. I jumped back.

'What's wrong with you?'

'Look, I'm sick of you making smart remarks about my weight and bullying me about those exercises. I hate exercises and I don't seem to have any time to read any more.'

'But, don't you know I'm only teasing you? I love your body.' Colette put her hand on my leg.

'Well I'm not a stone!'

'Don't talk!' Colette put her finger on my lips. I held my breath and kept still. Colette pulled my body close to hers. I could feel every part of her long body. It was nice. I lay still and waited. Colette lay on top of me and kissed me on the mouth. I let her close my eyelids with her plump fingers and shivered as she pulled up my night dress. I felt her lips on my stomach and I kind of let go everything. Her hands ran all over my body and she rubbed my feet until they tingled. It was nicer than a trance. She ran her hands up my legs very slowly and her fingers crept inside my thighs.

I thought about those bubbles of fat Colette said were between Miss Pole's legs. I opened my eyes to see the dormitory bright in moonlight and Colette's head buried between my thighs. I screamed at the top of my voice.

'You bitch!' hissed Colette, jumping onto the floor. 'We're for it now.'

A door slammed and the dormitory was windy with whispers. It sounded as if all the girls were twisting straw hats through their fingers.

Colette wrenched my nightdress down roughly, but it stayed in a ruffle around my hips as I lay there stupidly listening to the rush of noises.

'Pull it down, get under the fucking covers.'

Colette pushed at me and I hauled myself under the bedclothes. The yellow curtains whisked back as Colette was belting her tartan dressing gown around her waist. Sister Peter stood there with a torch. The funny thing was all I could think was that the torch didn't suit Peter. She'd have looked better with a candle. But she had her shawl wrapped around her head. She still looked like a Real Irish Mother. She gave Colette a funny look.

'What is all the commotion?' she said, hanging on to her shawl, holding it firmly under her chin. In case we saw her hair.

'I don't know, Sister,' Colette said. 'I've just come in to see what was up. She must have had a bad dream. Did you, Grace?'

'I don't know. It was something awful shocking,' I said. I was feeling really weird. Like someone had put plastic paper over my ear drums. Everything seemed muffled.

Colette placed a hand on my head, 'Well it doesn't feel hot. The poor thing must be frightened on her own.'

'Miss MacSweeney, there is more to this as you well know and I have every intention of getting to the bottom of it.' I jumped with fright to hear Peter speaking. She sounded like the rest of the nuns. She didn't beat her breast or clench her fist like an Irish mother. She sounded just like the rest of them. And really cross.

Suddenly I was crying, 'I saw the devil in the mirror!' A sheet of tears appeared on my face. Peter crossed herself.

'Jesus, Mary, and Saint Joseph. Don't say that, child!'

I sobbed. Out of control. My voice got louder, 'In the mirror, Sister. He was awful with red horns and a snake coming out of his throat.'

'Calm down, Grace.' Peter blessed herself again and backed away from my bed. 'Get her a glass of water,' she hissed to Colette.

Colette calmly poured a glass of water from the tap and handed it to me. She patted Peter on the back. The nun shook her hand off with a shudder and looked at the mirror anxiously. She looked like she was going to make some terrible prophecy. I drank down the water and my shoulders stopped shaking.

'Now Grace, I know you must be frightened on your own but you're a big girl. You must be brave. It's all in your imagination.' Peter gave a few more fortune-telling looks into the mirror.

'I'm always telling her that, Sister,' Colette said, sounding very down to earth and capable.

'Has this happened before?'

'Just once,' I said, carefully.

'Now, Grace, we won't say anything to anybody about this. The devil loves attention, it's a well known fact. You're going to have to take no notice of him!'

'Okay,' I said.

Peter gave Colette a fierce look. 'And not a word out of you to anyone! This must go no further than these four walls. If the Reverend Mother knew, things could become very hard and you would probably have to leave. It could involve the bishop.' Calling Jesus, Mary and Joseph again and making me promise to say my prayers, she left quickly. She looked at the ceiling before she left. Her eyes were tragic.

Colette followed.

I called out, 'Goodnight,' expecting a grateful look for my brain wave, but Colette snarled at me viciously. 'Something awful shocking!' and shut the curtains abruptly.

It was as if she had hit me. The curtains fell down and I couldn't stop crying for ages.

The next morning my left middle finger was throbbing.

I met Colette on the way to Mass.

'My finger is really sore.'

'Is it?' Colette said, examining the mole on her elbow.

'It really is.' I looked at Colette, 'What's wrong?'

'Nothing.'

'Have I done something?'

'You've done nothing,' Colette said bitterly. As we walked down the brass staircase in silence, we met Peter, carrying a bundle of steel hot water bottles. She crossed to the other side of the stairs.

· *Twelve* ·

That night, Colette moved back to her own bed.

I felt a storm of anger in my chest as she moved out her toothbrush and pyjamas with a careless and wounded air. God, I was the one who'd put herself on the line. And every time I remembered Colette's head lying between my legs, my cheeks burned.

My legs were too fat.

Sister Peter gave me weird looks. Haunted looks. The looks of someone who knew something dire was going to happen. I couldn't take it. If I saw her coming I'd double back on the corridor. Once I saw her at the end of the top corridor and before I'd time to turn back, I saw her whisk around and vanish down the back stairs. She never came near my cubicle after lights out. I could do what I liked. I played patience by the light of the full moon on the wooden window sill and finished my peardrops while my fingers throbbed and throbbed. The fingertip had become large, red and shiny and I wrapped it in a wet cold flannel that dripped down my nightdress.

Colette spoke to Trish and ignored me. The hardest part was pretending not to care. Especially when I heard her making a racket in Trish's cubicle every night. Sometimes they were really quiet and that was worse. I was sure that Colette was rubbing the crease on the inside of Trish's elbow.

I didn't like to say anything about my finger to Trish. I didn't want her to think that I was looking for sympathy. But the first day of the Christmas holidays, she copped and she was really nice to me. Helped me carry my suitcase to the iron gate. Sister Carmel had wrapped my finger in a big white bandage. It felt like I had another heart, beating in my finger. Under the bandage my finger looked like a lollipop.

My mother wore sunglasses. 'The winter sun is deadly,' she said. But I knew it was because she had been crying. She always cried at Christmas. 'It looks a bit red,' she said after I'd unwrapped the bandage. Then she frowned at the road to show that she was serious about her driving.

My finger got more painful. My mother had a crisis. She said if she had to cook the Christmas dinner again she would go off her head. But we always went to Auntie Catherine's place. Delia made really nice potato croquettes. I did the donkey stuff like putting crosses on the stems of the Brussels sprouts and chopping onions for the stuffing. I was glad to have Delia though, because she made a big effort for Christmas. She put up all the decorations five days before Christmas and went to great rounds over the Christmas tree. She even got my mother and Auntie Catherine to play Scrabble on Christmas Day.

Auntie Catherine wasn't much good at doing things herself but she did everything that Delia told her. She spent hours making a wreath of holly for the front door. Her small hands were red and scratched from the prickles but she was happy. She hummed *Jingle Bells*.

'There's nothing sadder than Christmas songs,' my mother said. Auntie Catherine shut up straight away.

My mother cut her finger getting the mince pies out of the deep freeze early Christmas morning. We heard the ghastly cry from the back kitchen.

Delia was the first out, 'Oh Auntie! Your poor finger.'

'I'm okay, honestly. Fine, well maybe I need a bandage.'

Delia had to link her arm and she protested all the way to the armchair by the fire. I had even more work to do, while Delia fussed and bandaged my mother's finger. And that was how my mother managed to spend all Christmas morning sitting down drinking sherry. Too weak to go to Mass of course. 'And I'd give my two eyes to be going with you.'

We had to leave her looking comfortable while we sat through Father Byrne's long mass. It was freezing. I felt the radiators. They weren't even switched on.

I didn't want to complain about my finger. I thought that everybody would see what a terrible state it was in. That they would stop me from doing the vegetables and make me sit down and rest. But they didn't notice my painful winces as I worked bravely.

My mother's bandage was bigger.

The day we were due to leave Auntie Catherine's house, I took the bandage off and showed them the yellow and green. My nail all funny coloured and lifting up from the bed.

'Good God!' Delia held my hand delicately.

'Whitlows they used to call them in my time,' said Auntie Catherine. 'I'll make you a poultice.'

'No, no, no,' said my mother. 'No, no we'll get the new G.P. to look at it. Dr Stoke. He's as keen as a knife. Ahead in his field!'

'Man of Science!' she said as we went into the shiny new surgery. The surgery was very bright.

I went through a red door to see Dr Stoke. He wore a black shirt and a brown moustache. After examining my finger, he shouted 'Christ!' and dragged me back out the red door to the waiting room. 'Mrs Jones,' he said, 'I'm very much afraid that the infection is in the bone. She may lose the finger.'

My mother stood up for a moment and then collapsed back into the chair. 'How will I survive?' she sobbed, tears bubbling down her cheeks. The other G.P. came out of a yellow door and fussed over her. He patted my mother's shoulder and Dr Stoke put a box of lavender-coloured Kleenex on her lap.

'*I'm a widow*!'

Dr Stoke gave me a glass of water and two huge white tablets. And then grabbed them back.

'Better not. We're sending you to hospital now. They may operate straight away.' He grabbed his purple telephone. He didn't look like a real doctor, more like the type of doctor you'd see in a film. Acting in an emergency. I was the emergency. My mother wished that she was.

My finger hadn't been as painful since it went green and yellow. It was worse when it was red. But I wasn't going to tell Dr Stoke that. I held my finger in my lap. It was so big and sore-looking. I couldn't help thinking wouldn't Delia get a shock. But best of all was thinking about Colette's terrible remorse. I hardly noticed the anaesthetist giving me the injection in the operating theatre. Just slid down that lovely dizzy slide, surrounded by people wearing sea-coloured tunics.

· Thirteen ·

I didn't lose my finger. They sliced the top off and said it would grow back in time. And when I returned to school I was put in a different dormitory. It was a shock. I was in with a load of first-years.

Colette didn't come to meet me. Trish was waiting at the iron gate to help carry my case. I tried to take it back, but she insisted. I didn't mention Colette.

When Trish opened the door to my new dormitory, I noticed Colette straight away. She had grown thinner and was swinging herself off the rope that pulled open the big window. I could see her long legs all the way up to her lemon knickers. My heart went mad. She jumped off the rope with an almighty pound on the floor.

'Very impressive,' she said to my bandaged finger which I held high in the air.

She tightened her lip, 'And you've got a very sympathetic nurse. Aren't you lucky! I'd like to stay and chat but I'm afraid I've got a lot of study to do for the Easter tests. I suppose you'll be excused, seeing as you're a semi-invalid.'

She slammed out the door.

'Don't take any notice,' Trish said. 'She's just guilty.'

'It doesn't look like that to me.'

'Colette always looks for attention, no matter what is wrong with her.'

'Well, she's not getting any from me.'

I wished Trish would go away. I wanted to cry.

Trish pushed me down on the bed. 'Now you just lie back and let me do everything.'

I lay down and Trish rubbed my forehead gently. I looked at her yellowy white skin that was so clear, it looked like plastic. 'Yellow plastic,' I whispered.

Trish ran the cold tap and soaked my green flannel. 'You need to cool down.' She laid the ice-cold flannel reverently across my forehead. 'Show me where to put your stuff,' she said, opening the case.

Trish hung up my uniforms and blouses, folded my jumpers and stacked my soap, talc and shampoo around the wash basin. She took a bottle of eau de cologne from her locker and rubbed it into my wrists. The smell reminded me of my mother. Sweet and half sick. My stomach churned. Maybe Colette would never speak to me again.

A picture of Saint Therese of the Little Flower hung over the mantelpiece. There were only eight beds. The fireplace was black and cold-looking. Blocked up.

'Colette wouldn't apologise or anything in front of me,' Trish said, when she was going.

Sister Carmel came in and shut the door quietly behind her. 'I hope you won't be too lonely.' She patted my shoulder. 'Try to make the best of it. They're nice girls in the Little Flower. I'm sure everything will work out for the best in the end.'

She walked around, dusting and straightening chairs. She was shy and I didn't know what to say to her. Her black nylon housecoat scraped against her habit and she made kind of dry sniffing noises that were really nice.

'And don't forget to take your iron tablets, we can't have you fading away. You've lost too much weight.'

Carmel seemed cross about me getting thin. She sat on my bed and crossed her soft ankles. Her nylon housecoat scratched slightly as she folded her arms. I watched the silver crucifix move on her chest as she breathed.

'Sister, is this punishment?'

'How could you think that?'

'I don't know.'

'Well, I'm sorry you feel like that. This is my dormitory and I'm pleased that you're going to be here to take charge. Offer it up to God and take care of those small little first-years.'

I drew the curtains before the first-years arrived and washed quickly. I took out the green nightdress that my mother bought for me when I went into hospital. It was slinky and went in at the bottom like a mermaid's tail. Colette might come round to apologise after lights out. I thought that she might like it. I didn't leave my cubicle. Kept the curtains tightly drawn. I couldn't bear talking to the first-years.

The bandage on my finger was sodden. It got wet every time I washed. It had to be dressed by a medical person. I couldn't change it myself. So I held it over the radiator to get it dry. The lights went off suddenly just as I was making my way into bed. I fell over in the dark. There were titters from around the dormitory. I stared laughing myself and then I remembered what Carmel had said. I didn't want her to catch me talking already.

'Sshhh, it's the ghost of Sister Mary Lelia, if you don't keep quiet she'll come in.'

The giggles died away and Brenda Driscoll with the red hair called out, 'Who's Sister Mary Lelia.'

'She walks these corridors every night, calling for her lost love.'

'God!' gasped a small voice from the corner. 'What happened to her?'

'She was a beautiful young girl whose family made her enter as a lay sister because they couldn't afford a dowry.'

'What colour hair had she?' asked the small girl in the corner.

'Blonde, yes blonde, sun-ripened hair. She had the most beautiful hair. Her sweetheart had gone to America to earn his fortune. He was very poor as well.'

'Was she waiting for him?' Brenda asked.

'Oh yes, this is the hard part, you see. The family stuck her in the convent the minute he was gone and she had to scrub stone floors on her bare knees and the Reverend Mother used to put nettles in her rubber gloves.'

'Why?' sighed the small voice.

'Because it was good for her to suffer.'

'Wow,' said a deep voice in the other corner.

'All the time she was a postulant, she prayed for him to come back. And every time she prayed for him to come back, the Reverend Mother made her stand in the river for a whole night.'

'Jesus Christ!'

'Don't use the Holy Name, Brenda.'

'But how did she know that Sister Lelia was praying for her lover?'

'She had ways of knowing,' I said, peering at my watch. Colette might come soon. I hurried on, 'Anyway, the day she took her final vows, he returned. He burst into the chapel, dressed as a cowboy.'

'Why as a cowboy?'

'Because he'd been working in the Wild West.'

'Did he pull a gun out?' asked the deep voice.

'Oh, don't be silly. Of course he didn't. It was a convent for God's sake. Anyway she was there, dressed all in white as a bride of Christ and the priest just putting the ring on her finger. They'd cut off all her beautiful golden hair and it was all over the floor of the chapel. She turned around just as he was leaving with his hands over his face and fell into a swoon.' I stopped and listened. I thought that I could hear Colette's footsteps. I waited a few moments.

'Well?' said the deep voice.

'The nuns never saw her alive again.'

'Why?'

I stopped again and listened. 'She slit her wrists that night and she's been haunting the place ever since.'

'Oh no!'

'I don't believe you.'

'Why not?'

'Because if he was a cowboy, he'd never have gone away quietly.'

'Truth is stranger than fiction,' I said, and listened again.

'That's weird about the hair isn't it?' Brenda said. 'I wonder what they do with all the hair they cut off?'

'They sell it to wigmakers,' the deep voice said.

'That's enough. You only attract ghosts with that kind of speculation. The next person to speak gets a fine of fifty pence.'

The whispers trickled away slowly and everything became quiet again. I waited for Colette but she didn't come. I took out a flashlamp and tried to read under the blankets. But the writing on the pages swam into black waves of disappointment.

· Fourteen ·

The next day, I went back to Doctor Buckley to get my finger dressed. Sister Carmel came with me, 'You need someone steady.'

And it was much safer this way. Dr Buckley couldn't be doing anything dodgy, like putting us into a car with Jerome. I really liked walking with Carmel. We didn't talk much, but it didn't matter. Everybody smiled at us. I didn't even feel like sweets when I passed Smarts.

The weather got grey as we came near Castle Road. Clouds just seemed to gather over Dr Buckley's house. It was the same the last time I'd been there. The time I went with Colette. Carmel knocked on the door. Her fist hardly made a sound. He couldn't possibly hear her knock. Of course I couldn't tell her to knock more loudly, but I was a bit annoyed with her for being patient and gentle. I had a faint but persistent desire to shake Sister Carmel. I fought it back.

'Oh, all his flowers are gone.' Carmel said.

'Did he have flowers?'

'Oh, yes. When Mrs Buckley was alive. They used to win prizes.'

'Did she do the flowers?'

'No, he did.'

The door creaked open, 'I was getting worried that ye weren't going to come at all,' Dr Buckley said. His face looked more purple than before and he had a metal bowl of stingy solution for my finger.

'You needn't bother with it if it's too much for you,' he said, looking at my face. I put my finger in quickly. God, he was careless. I had to look out for myself. I could get gangrene or anything. I hoped the bandages were clean. Jerome could have been fingering them. Or trying them on. I felt sick thinking about it.

Dr Buckley spilled the antiseptic powder everywhere, but he was good at winding the bandage. Tight but not too much. It felt nice. Firm and dry. I rubbed my bandaged finger against my cheek. I liked having a bandage. I would miss it when my finger was better.

Mrs A. was on her holidays. 'I packed her off to Ballybunion for two weeks. There's nothing like it. Great freedom.'

'I've never been there,' Carmel turned to me. 'Have you, Grace?'

'I'm not talking about Ballybunion. I'm talking about my own freedom. I can do what I like!'

Carmel went quiet. I didn't blame her. It was a really embarrassing thing to say. It wasn't fair to Mrs A. and it made me think about what he wanted to do on his own. I supposed he went drinking or something. Or maybe he lured young girls into his surgery. But then he brought us down to the kitchen and laid the table all by himself. He took half-squashed chocolate cake out of a box and I thought that he was fairly nice after all.

I thought that it was great that Carmel was getting served. She looked really awed. He heated the teapot and everything. He knew what to do.

I stuck out my little finger again as I held the china

teacup, and the three of us made intelligent conversation. I was afraid for a while that he'd mention Jerome. But he was only interested in the convent. He asked about all the nuns. Even Sister Peter. And especially Sister Assumpta. Carmel told him that Sister Assumpta was going off to the missions. It was a sudden decision.

'Uganda is it? By God! She's a fine young woman,' Doctor Buckley said admiringly.

I went red with embarrassment, he was so shameless. And then tried to cover the redness by putting my hand up to my face.

'Are you worried about Sister Assumpta?' Carmel asked me.

'Are there tigers in Uganda?' I said evasively.

'Ah, tigers! Tigers! She'll have to watch out for the tigers all right, especially the black ones.' Doctor Buckley started laughing low in his belly. Really stupid. He suddenly stopped and looked at me very seriously, 'Do you know this one,

Tiger! Tiger! Burning bright
  In the forest of the night
What immortal hand or eye
DARE (he roared) DARE frrrrame thy fearrrful
  symmetry.'

'I do,' I said.

'Tell me who wrote it and I'll give you five bob.'

'Mmmn,' I hummed, wanting to know the answer so badly that I couldn't think at all.

'Answer me now! Come on, come on. It's easy. For five bob remember.'

The embarrassment was killing me. An easy answer and I couldn't even get it!

'Was it Yeats?'

'Wrong, wrong, wrong as Moll Bell! What's wrong with you at all? Sure, it was Blake.'

'Oh, that's right,' I said foolishly.

'Here's the prize, anyway.' Dr Buckley spun the money across the table.

We didn't stay long after that. Carmel had to get the suppers ready. She put on her black raincoat and pulled on her black cotton gloves.

'You'll not put your foot on the pavement without an escort,' Doctor Buckley said, holding on to Carmel's arm. 'Stay there.' He went out the back door.

I thought that he was going to get Jerome again. But he was just bringing his Morris Oxford around to the front. Colette and I had voted Morris Oxfords the very worst car after Morris Minors and Anglias.

He had no fear on the road. Kept turning around to say things. That was partly Carmel's fault for not sitting in the front seat.

'I've got a tiger in my tank.'

He started his belly laugh again. We were really mortified. You could see Carmel was just praying for him to shut up.

Along the road to the convent, the bungalows sandwiched the blue sea. It was a fine day, but that made the salmon-pink garage look worse. I held my freshly bound finger to my nose and smelled the new bandage.

'Ah, God, a fine day for January. Crispy blue. Look at that sky.' As he turned into the convent avenue, he was still talking over his shoulder and exclaiming about the sky, youth and poetry. Then there was a horrible bang. A jolt. Time seemed to stop.

Dr Buckley wound down the window.

'Where did you come from?' he shouted down at the ground.

'Where the fuck do you think you're going, driving

with your head facing the wrong direction?' a voice said, speaking very slowly. Ironically, I giggled.

'Young man, have a bit of respect and get up and speak properly. There's a religious sister and a girl in this car.'

'Well, you didn't show much respect for me, driving all over me. I don't know if I'm able to get up. I've an awful fucking pain in my knee.' The voice was beginning to sound kind of familiar.

'The young blackguard!' said Dr Buckley to us. 'Let me at him!' He opened the door and got out. Carmel nudged me. We got out as well.

It was Johnny. I didn't need even to see the big black motorbike sprawled on the grass beside him. He looked the same as Colette. Except his hair was longer. And he didn't have Spock eyebrows. But he still looked fierce devilish. He winked at me.

'Sorry, Sister, about the language but I'm not in the best of shape.' He spoke so slowly. Kind of sinister. It was very nice. Not a bit sorry really.

It drove Dr Buckley mad. 'Get up, you young rascal. There's nothing wrong with you.'

Johnny got up slowly. His legs were long and thin. He wore tight blue Levis. So faded they were nearly white. I could hardly look at him, he was so brilliant. I wished that I was wearing a longer uniform. So that he couldn't see *my* legs.

He limped over to his bike and tried to pull it up. Dr Buckley helped him. Dying to get rid of him. Get away from the scene of the accident. Johnny took his time.

'And what are you doing hanging around a girl's school?' Dr Buckley had a disgusted and suspicious voice.

'Same as you.'

Dr Buckley went red. 'And what is that supposed to mean?'

Johnny gave him a slow look and took out a packet of cigarettes.

'Visiting.'

'Why?'

'He's Colette's brother,' I said. I was afraid Dr Buckley would have him arrested or something.

'Thank you,' Johnny smiled at me. His front tooth was crooked.

'Do you need to come back to the convent?' asked Carmel.

Johnny put his hand up. 'No, I'm okay. I won't come back. I've seen Colette and I suppose I'll just hobble on my way.'

'Well if you're sure.' Carmel sounded relieved.

'Of course he's sure. Young healthy fellow. No need to hang around.'

Johnny took ages getting on the bike and he had to put his foot down on the accelerator loads of times before it got started.

'Lean on it, lean on it, man,' Dr Buckley said. 'God, these long-haired hairy mollies, they're not men at all.'

Johnny looked straight at me.

'Say Ciao to Colette.'

· *Fifteen* ·

'Tell me again,' Colette said.

We were lying on my bed, the first-years were asleep. I had told them another ghost story to shut them up. They were getting addicted. Colette was rubbing the crease on the inside of my elbow.

'What colour was Dr Buckley's face?'

'Puce.'

'I love it! I can't wait to talk to Johnny. Oh Buckley's such an eedjit.' Colette put her hand on my leg.

I didn't mind her hand on my leg any more. 'Tell me about Johnny.'

'What do you want to know?'

'What size are his Levis?'

'Thirty.'

'Does he really listen to the Sex Pistols?'

'No.'

'Oh.'

'Well I was only showing off when I said it to you.'

'Who are they?'

'Punks. And the lead singer is called Johnny Rotten.'

'Johnny's bound to have their album by now, isn't he?'

'Yes, I'm sure.' Colette started kissing me. I thought

about Johnny every time she touched me. It was really brilliant.

Colette was doing her exercises. 'I'm fucking well behind. Still at least I've been sick as a dog all week. That has to count for something.' She held out her hand really high and touched it with her foot. Then started twisting her waist so fast I was dizzy looking at her.

'With what?'

'The gawks!'

'The what?'

'Vomiting of course. Haven't you heard of the gawks, girl?'

She pulled my plait which was lying on the pillow. And got into bed with me, forgetting to do her exercises. We were both fierce excited since we had started talking again.

'It must be awful having the gawks.'

'Feel my stomach, it's caved in.' She guided my hand across her stomach with cold fingers. My hands seemed to burn on her cool skin as I felt the shallow bowl between her hip bones.

'That feels nice,' she said, and pressed my hand hard on her stomach.

'Is my hand too hot?' I asked.

'No, it's fucking fantastic.'

'What does Johnny do for a living?'

'Nothing.'

'Nothing?'

'He doesn't believe in it.'

'What?'

'Being exploited.'

'Isn't he bored?'

'God, no. He reads piles. Even more than you. And he grows cannabis plants.'

I didn't know what cannabis plants were. Colette lay on top of me. I liked it now. I thought about Johnny. Those whitish Levis. His long hair. His voice. I didn't feel too embarrassed. As long as nobody found out. Besides Colette had promised not to put her head between my legs again. We spent the whole night together. Fell asleep, talking, about three. I got such a fright when I woke up and saw the grey dawn.

'Carmel! Carmel will be here at any minute!' I hissed at Colette and watched her, with my plait in my mouth, as she struggled into her pyjamas.

'It's okay, it's okay. It's only quarter past six. I've got a quarter of an hour to get back to Joseph's.'

It was really romantic. I held Colette very tight for a minute. 'I love your white pyjamas,' I whispered, as she went to the door.

I had to fix the first-year's berets, before they went to Mass at seven o'clock. They fidgeted and moaned about their berets looking like soup plates.

'I look like someone out of *The Quiet Man*' Brenda was giving out. I didn't say anything but I thought that she did look like someone you'd see dangling her legs over the side of a jaunting car or sitting on a donkey. In postcards of the Real Ireland. I told her she didn't look a bit like anyone from *The Quiet Man.* Someone had to keep her spirits up.

I told them that first-year heads were always too small for their berets and that they would grow into them. They went off to Mass, wishing the years away.

'Mine is too *small* for me,' corrected the deep-voiced girl, before clumping out defiantly.

I knew who she was now, Geraldine White.

'There's thanks for you,' I shouted after her. 'I'm late for Mass now.'

I ran out, tying my sash as the bell was going for Mass. I saw Colette on the brass staircase. 'Can't stop.

Getting the gawks,' she said and I looked after her proudly.

We were having a retreat. It was all being aware of God and trying to make you feel guilty. We had to keep total silence. I went with Trish to the nuns' graveyard and we talked at the top of our voices and looked at all the graves, shivering at the inscriptions about the nuns who'd died young.

Colette was in bed, sick again. She told Sister Carmel that she had the gawks. Sister Carmel was taken aback by Colette's new word and sent her off to the dormitory without even checking her temperature.

Trish and I went down to the stream and sat down on the bank. It was cold and damp. We spread our gabardine coats on the grass. I had a book called *I am Alive* by Kitty Hart. She'd been in a concentration camp. We were glued to it. There were pictures of skulls and piles of false teeth. Mass graves. It was really sad. I couldn't wait to tell the first-years all about it when we were going to bed. Body fat was melted down for soap and candles, bones carved into paperweights. There was nothing too horrible. I couldn't help feeling a bit envious, though, when Kitty Hart was describing how thin she got. Not all the time of course. Not at the end when her teeth were falling out and everything. If only you could get sent to a concentration camp just for a few weeks to get really thin. Escape before your teeth got loose.

I said that the nuns were just the same as the Nazis except that the nuns wore veils and that was the only difference. At the really bad bits we cried and clenched our fists and said what we would do with the Nazis if we got hold of them.

There were pictures of women running naked into the concentration camp. I thought that was really mean. Some of the Jewish women were lovely looking. I wished I was Jewish. Trish said that she would loan me *The Diary of Anne Frank.*

'I hate my thighs,' I said.

'You're going to end up like Colette if you don't watch it,' Trish said.

'And what's wrong with that?'

'Well, if you want to end up looking like someone out of a concentration camp, I suppose there's nothing wrong with it.'

God, I *wanted* to look like someone out of a concentration camp. Spooky. Wasted. Spiritual-looking. I stood up and gathered my coat. I shrugged my shoulders, 'I've got miles to go before I'm anyway near as thin as Colette. I mean she gets sick as well.'

'Huh, gets sick,' Trish snorted. 'Very convenient.'

We folded our coats over our arms and walked back towards the school. When we passed the nuns' graveyard, a spectral hand came over the wall. 'Help!' said a thin voice and then giggled. We weren't stunned even for a minute.

'We aren't scared,' I told her.

'Oh, you're getting very bold, Miss Jones,' Colette said in Colm's voice.

At the iron gate we waited for her to come out. She put her arm around my waist and I kissed her on the lips. A cold sliver of wind sliced at the bottom of my skirt. All those dead nuns, buried in their Child of Mary cloaks, pursing their skeleton mouths disapprovingly.

'I'm very weak,' Colette groaned, leaning on my arm as we streeled back to the school. 'Worn out from the gawks.'

· *Sixteen* ·

Johnny had a first-class honours science degree. 'Could have any job he wanted.' I was back in the honours maths class. So was Colette. She was useless, but determined to stick it out. We were all doing science subjects. I liked algebra because you just got on with the job and worked it out. It wasn't the sort of thing where you had to think about water travelling through pipes of certain diameters and into tanks, and chew your pencil. Those kind of problems made my mind wander. So did those physics problems where bullets were ricocheting off tree trunks and travelling at all kinds of velocity. I liked doing derivations though, and did them over and over on scraps of paper. Feeling advanced. Imagining Johnny's eyes were on me.

It occurred to me then that I liked English too much and I'd better concentrate on science. Delia said that it was much safer because there was only one answer. It made me feel sensible and practical. It wasn't a flighty type of subject. It was impressive and clever. Steady. A good sign of my character. I thought about giving up acting. I didn't say this to Colette, but she had stopped calling us artistes.

If I became scientific, it would change my life. My

mother might think that I was mysterious. I would be very wise and would be able to talk knowledgeably on technical subjects. I would know how to fix cars and would build radios. I saw myself in a white coat, holding bunsen burners, wearing goggles, making strides in the field of science. Helping Johnny with his cannabis. Discovering a new element for the periodic table. Saving thousands of lives. With Johnny and Colette working tirelessly beside me. Colette wasn't very good though. Funny that she hadn't got Johnny's mathematical genius. She could keep the laboratory tidy. Rinse out the pipettes and burettes.

I began to study very hard. Everybody noticed. Which was a bit of a pain, because I didn't want to get called a swot. I lost weight. Not enough people noticed. I ate very little. Trish didn't know how I survived on one slice of bread a day. I tried to explain how enjoyable it was being hungry, but she didn't understand. She thought that Colette and I were mad. I thought Colette was a small bit mad, but I definitely wasn't.

And Colette had brilliant will power. She didn't even need to eat, just kept going. And studying. Got up early every morning to wash her hair. It was all fluffy and halo-like in the refectory every morning as she sat pretending to eat a bowl of cornflakes. The nuns were watching her. She was supposed to be trying to eat more. But Colette always managed to sling her breakfast in the bin when nobody was looking. All the first-years thought Colette was really brilliant.

This was the best time I had with Colette. We didn't do anything. We just hugged each other and slept together. And she always rubbed the crease on the inside of my elbow when I asked her to.

'How many pairs of Levis has Johnny?'

'Four. Oh no, it's just three. He's got a pair of Wranglers as well.'

'And what colours are his check shirts.'

'They're all either red or blue. Oh and he's got one really dark navy one.'

'I'd say it really suits him.'

'Mmmm, he's not that great though. Sometimes he gets huge pimples on the back of his neck.'

'Really?'

'Yeah, and on his back as well.'

'Gee.'

'I have to squeeze them.'

'No!'

'He'd beat me up if I didn't.'

'He doesn't really beat you.'

'He doesn't half! And he's got about four girlfriends.'

Conversations about Johnny always started off nice, but they ended up horrible.

'You'll have to learn to like sex if you want Johnny.'

'I don't want Johnny.'

'You do. You do.'

'I don't.'

'Swear you'll never go out with him then.'

'I do.'

'Go on, say it properly. Go down on your knees. Here's Trish's prayer book.'

The floor was freezing. 'I swear by the almighty God.'

'And all the Saints and Angels in Heaven.'

'And all the Saints and Angels in Heaven that I'll never go out with Johnny.'

'I wouldn't keep you to it. You don't believe all that rubbish anyway.'

Colette gave me a book about sex. It was really embarrassing. She said that I had to read it. That I had to start masturbating. That I'd have to lose my virginity before I went out with Johnny.

'I don't want to go out with Johnny!'

'We'll take the saddle off Peter's bicycle. And then you'll have to sit on it. It hurts like mad. But then it's all over and you'll be free!'

I liked Johnny. I thought about him a lot. But I didn't dare think about going out with him. He was too good-looking, too sophisticated. He wouldn't be bothered with me. But Colette said that she was being practical. She said I wasn't being scientific. She made me borrow *Our Bodies Ourselves.*

I had to read it while she plucked my eyebrows. She did my eyebrows and her own once a week. I hated it. She put vaseline on my eyebrows first. It was supposed to make it easier. But it couldn't possibly have been more painful. The first time Colette did it, I screamed so loud Carmel came running in without her veil. I had to tell her that I had had a nightmare and she stayed sitting on the bed for ages, looking like a shorn lamb. And racking her brains for comforting things to say. Colette was underneath the bed, prodding my mattress with her tweezers.

'You have to suffer to be beautiful. There's crowds of girls out there fighting for Johnny. And they're not virgins,' Colette said, later, when she was doing the other eyebrow. I held *Our Bodies Ourselves* against my chest and said nothing, but I hated those girls.

· *Seventeen* ·

I began to get abscesses again. They became bigger and more severe. The strange part was I got used to pain, it was like dieting. Conquering the weak side of myself, like when I took cold baths with Colette. The shock was terrible, but then you felt very strong.

Trish brought me books from the library when I was in bed. And dusted my locker. Tidied out my wardrobe. She even embroidered a small cloth to put on top of my locker. Colette thought that was awful. Carmel kept admiring it. Carmel was so nice to me. Colette said she hated her.

'I don't know how you could possibly say anything against Carmel. She could have got you in trouble loads of time but she didn't.'

'She's afraid of me because I'm the millionaire's daughter.'

'Well, I'm the daughter of the poor widow and she doesn't say anything to me either.'

'That's because you're her pet.'

'I'm not.'

'She's sex-crazed,' Colette leered.

The dormitory door opened and Brenda Driscoll came in.

'Shut up.'

'I won't.

Brenda gave us a funny look and came over to my bed. 'How are you today?'

'Fine,' I said weakly to show that I was putting up a good show.

'I don't know how you stand it here all day.'

'It's all right.' I gave a sigh.

'Brenda?' Colette gave me a mean look.

'Yes?'

'Do you know what sex-crazed is?'

'Yes.'

'What is it?'

'You are.'

Colette started laughing. Rolling over and over on top of my legs. I was raging. Imagine rolling over a sick person's legs!

'There's no God.'

'I know,' said Brenda. Her red hair was an exact round ball and I thought that it was special hair and she didn't look like someone from *The Quiet Man* any more. Not even like someone from a postcard of the Real Ireland.

'How do you know that there's no God?'

'My father told me. He's an atheist.'

Colette was really upscuttled, 'And what are you doing here so?'

'Because my mother wanted me to come and I'm related to Benedicta.'

Sister Peter loved my abscesses. She poulticed them in boiling water and that was dreadful. But she liked squeezing them as well. Carmel didn't like it, but Peter always managed to get hold of me somehow. Once when I had a boil on my chin, she backed me up against the pantry door and squeezed until the tears ran down my face. Her nylon coat stank of turnips.

I was always relieved when Carmel came back. She took care of my ear abscesses. Peter wasn't allowed. Even if she was I wouldn't have let her. Carmel was the only person that I let near my ears. They were the worst.

Carmel heated the olive oil in a little crucible in the huge kitchen range. I was nervous waiting for it.

'Sister, Sister, I think it's time to take it out. It's going to be really boiling.'

'But I've only just put it in, Grace.'

I had to lie with my head on one side on the kitchen table while Carmel poured the olive oil into my ear. Sometimes I felt a shock inside my ear. I hated being in that vulnerable position, but I suffered it for Sister Carmel.

Doctor Buckley increased the strength of my antibiotics. It didn't stop the abscesses. I spent more and more time in the dormitory reading novels, feeling guilty because I wasn't masturbating or studying physics. Colette gave me a book about a man who was in love with the earth. He spent some of his time lying in the earth trying to kiss it and get into the ground.

Don't forget to W! Colette had written on the inside of the back cover.

Then someone found an old copy of *Frankenstein* in the library. Everyone was reading it. I stayed up all night to finish it. I felt so sorry for the poor rejected monster and I hadn't a bit of sympathy for Frankenstein. It wasn't the monster's fault that Frankenstein had 'collected bones from Charnel-houses and disturbed with profane fingers, the tremendous secrets of the human frame'. He didn't ask to be born.

I cried for the monster isolated on Mont Blanc. I couldn't forget that icy river. His loneliness.

Then I read bits of it to the first years. The bits

about the monster's hideous yellow skin and the terrible chase through the frozen wastes.

The windows banged and the doors rattled. The wind was creepy coming down the chimney. I began to have nightmares about Peter chasing me with the kitchen knife threatening to cut off my finger.

Once I dreamt about Johnny and he was trying to squeeze my abscess. It was annoying to think I had only one dream about Johnny and I had an abscess in it.

Sometimes, Colette wouldn't sleep with me. 'You're getting too much attention. It's bad for you. You must suffer.'

Sometimes, I cried myself to sleep. I felt awful. Like a baby. And useless. Good only for reading novels.

Colette said that Johnny was building his own bike and he would drive down to see us when it was finished. 'He never wears a helmet.'

'Why not?'

'He believes if you die, you die. There's no point in trying to avoid it.'

'God, he's really wild.'

'He thinks you shouldn't give a damn about anything.'

'I agree with him. It's true.'

'And he doesn't allow his girlfriends to wear helmets either! And he goes twice as fast when he's going around a corner.'

Why did my stomach dip when she said it?

'And he never goes out with anyone who weighs more than seven stone.' Colette had reached seven stone on the scales. Her words rankled for ages afterwards. I was eight stone and away shorter.

· *Eighteen* ·

My abscesses came more often. Almost every week another one erupted. The poultices got more severe. Sister Paul came one evening and forcibly held my hand in the hottest water ever. The abscess burst the instant she removed my hand and I cried with the relief of the pressure. The fingernail fell off a few days later. By now I had a big collection of old fingernails which I kept in an empty vaseline jar in my bedside locker. Colette said they were brilliant.

I got abscesses in my ears, my nose and under my arm. Doctor Buckley told me the classic places were the axillae, the neck and the groin. I thought he enjoyed saying the word *groin.* I looked out the window when he said it. Colette said it would be a great place to get one. Because Peter wouldn't be able to squeeze it, then.

Sister Paul bought a huge jar of cod liver oil and plonked it on my table in the refectory. It was more like a barrel really and it had added malt. It smelt revolting, I went weak every time the lid was taken off. Three tablespoons a day, one with each meal. I couldn't manage even one. Colette said it was enough to give a horse the gawks.

'Try and take your tonic,' Carmel said, as if it was a lovely raspberry syrup or something.

Trish came up with the plan of transferring a tablespoon to an empty coffee jar at each meal. The first-years helped. Everyone felt really sorry for me. It was great. One of the leaving certs told me she would leave if she was made to take that tonic.

'It's not too bad,' I said.

'You're getting really thin,' the leaving cert said and I thanked her.

I couldn't keep anything else in my locker, it was full of 2oz Maxwell House jars full of sticky brown tonic. The liquid seeped out. It was everywhere. I had to wash my hands for ages after depositing another jar. The corridor began to stink of fish. Colm came around smelling.

Then Paul took all the first-years into a room and gave them a lecture. All about periods and developing bodies needing to be spotless. I was told to supervise the first-years in my dormitory. Make sure they were washing themselves.

I spent more and more time in the dormitory. Colette said I was like one of those half man half horse things. Except that I was half woman half bed. Carmel brought me such dainty trays. The nicest cakes and biscuits. Chocolate and lemon cake. College creams. I gave them all to Trish.

'You're mad,' Trish said, every time I gave her a custard slice or a doughnut.

Sometimes Colette would announce that we were having a *breakout* and we would eat all the stuff on my tray and order sweets from one of the town girls, as well. We always felt terrible afterwards. Colette usually got the gawks after a *breakout*. She was lucky. I had to lie awake imagining all the butter and sugar coating my hips and thighs in another horrible layer of blubbery fat.

Breakouts were usually followed by stringent dieting like eating nothing for a day. Colette never stopped giving advice. I always listened. Cigarettes were a must if you were dieting. I had to be seven stone too. I decided to get very serious about smoking.

We walked up to the farmyard after school one evening. It seemed like something out of a very old life. I'd forgotten about grass and old sheds. About wide spaces and the smell of cows. We passed the farm nuns swaddled in their black shawls. They didn't look up from their work as they bent over, looking like black stacks of material harvested from the land. I envied them. They never had to worry about being seven stone. Or pluck their eyebrows. It had to be nice if you only had to worry about God. And a place waiting for you in Heaven.

We said hello and they smiled shyly at us. Colette sang and gyrated as she walked and I wished she wouldn't do it in front of those nuns. I felt that they should be protected from the outside world at all costs. Colette told me not to be such an old fool.

I liked the old sheds. I liked the way they were overgrown and some of them were like cottages and you could imagine people living in them.

'Do you think people lived in these before the famine?'

I loved thinking about history. Especially bad history. It was really creepy.

'The people in these cottages died on coffin ships.'

'How do you know?' I hated being fooled. It was no good if Colette just made up a story to please me.

'No, seriously. Sister Assumpta told us in biology

class. You know when she goes off the point and can't stop talking.'

'Where was I?'

'Sick.' Colette took a deep breath. 'And afterwards other people came to live in them, but *they* ended up in America as well. Some of them were so ashamed they didn't tell anyone that they were going.'

'Why were they ashamed?'

'Because it was an awful failure like going bankrupt or something. They just left in the middle of the night. Left the house behind them. Listen to this one! My father told me this joke about a man who went up to Cork to buy his ticket for America. And he asked for a one-way ticket and the man at the ticket desk asked, "What is your destination?" And your man said, "Mind your own bloody business!" '

'That's awful sad.'

'You would think so. It's supposed to be funny.'

I wanted to go into one of the old cottages and sit down in the corner. To get a feeling. But Colette said that we had to press on. We passed through a large steel shed. It had a terrible smell.

'You can't beat silage,' Colette said contemptuously at the hankerchief I held over my nose. 'Take deep breaths. It's good for the lungs.'

Colette stopped at a pen and half a dozen black and white calves strained to look at us. Their brown eyes were massive with curiosity. They scratched and skittered around the pen, but never took their eyes off us.

'Aren't they sweet?' I said, my throat suddenly full. As if I were going to cry or something stupid.

'You are gone soft in the head. Come on, I'll give you a leg over.'

'We're not going in there.'

'It's the safest place, nobody'll see us.'

'But how do you know there isn't a bull in there?'

'For Jesus's sake, where have you lived all your life? If there was a bull in there, we'd recognise him very quick.'

I took the leg over and soon we were standing in the middle of the calves. They began pressing themselves against us, thinking they were getting food. Their solid bodies were half comforting half frightening.

'Get back, you dogs,' Colette said, fumbling for the cigarettes and matches.

It took ages to light the cigarettes in the wind. Colette tried loads of times, cupping her hand around the match. It was kind of nice for a while, dragging really hard and looking out at the fields. The farmyard was on a height and we could see right across the nuns' green fields which were scattered with bits of the old railway line.

I looked at Colette's hands. They were whitish when she clenched her fists. They weren't plump any more. Like they were when I came first. She was thin everywhere now. She was perfect.

The calves became more curious. One of them tried to lick my hand and he followed me around the pen. The more frantically I tried to get away, the more he flattened himself against me.

'Hit him a belt,' Colette said, carelessly. There was smoke pouring out her nostrils.

But I couldn't. He was really sad-looking.

Colette said things like, 'Ride them coyboy' and 'Weeha'. It was dreary smoking with nothing in your stomach and I felt queasy several times, especially when the calf breathed hotly into my face.

I climbed out first. Colette stayed in the pen, smoking one cigarette after another, even though she must have been feeling sick.

'You've got to harden yourself up,' she shouted out

at me, the calves grouped around her tall figure as if they were posing for a photograph.

'Don't annoy me,' I said, putting my head between my knees to try and get rid of the nausea.

'Why don't you just get sick? You could have a slice of bread for your tea then.'

I shook my head. I couldn't like cigarettes. I wished I could. Johnny liked Marlboro.

The nausea passed and some sunlight got trapped in the corner where I sat waiting for Colette. I felt the warmth beating on my jumper and threw back my head to warm my face.

'It's much nicer here,' I called to Colette.

'You burn up more fat out of the sun, because your body has to keep you warm. That sun is artificial heat.'

When we got back to the school, Sister Carmel had a letter from my mother. She was taking me to a consultant in Cork. Investigating my abscesses at last. I supposed I was an embarrassment to my mother as usual, filling up with horrible yellow pus every week. It was not a glamorous or romantic illness. No, it was not like being too thin. Mysterious.

· *Nineteen* ·

Easter came in March that year. The consultant said I would have to go into hospital for tests during the holidays and I thought that I heard him whisper something about diabetes to my mother. I was thrilled and I couldn't wait to tell Colette. I was sure to lose a load of weight in hospital.

I was going private this time. 'What's the point of paying V.H.I. if you can't take advantage?' said my mother.

Going private meant you had to have nuns. Which was a bit of a pain. The new hospital had all the same paraphernalia as Mayo, white plaster statues poised around the grounds and coloured statues in every alcove inside the building. It had the same smell of furniture polish, and my feet made the same hollow yet deep sound on the polished floors. The nuns looked different dressed in white habits and veils. Sometimes I would try and match each nun with one from Mayo, but there were always a few awkward individuals who wouldn't fit into the scheme. And there was nobody like Sister Carmel.

I shared my room with Mrs Dunne, a middle-aged fat woman who was always talking about golf and opera music. She didn't care if I knew anything about them or not. She never waited for my replies anyway. Lots of women came to see her and they all talked about golf and Frank Patterson the singer. They smiled condescendingly and asked me how I was. They turned up the television really loud when Frank Patterson came on and turned off the television during programmes that I liked.

One night when 'The Old Man and the Sea' was on television Mrs Dunne got out of bed and turned the television off. 'It's too depressing,' she said, 'I like something with a romantic interest.'

I looked at the white dot of light disappearing into the blank television screen and thought how I hated Mrs Dunne. A capitalist pig. I swore that when I grew up I wouldn't get fat and narrow-minded. I ate nothing.

'No wonder there isn't a pick of you there,' Mrs Dunne said.

She was always complaining about her weight. 'I wouldn't mind but I never eat.'

'Huh!' I said to myself.

That's what made me laugh about all her generation. They were always going on about the hardship during the war years. About how they cried when they saw a packet of tea. And broke down when they saw a pound of butter. But they hadn't a clue. *We* really knew what it was like to starve.

I lay on my bed in a long white nightdress and felt ethereal. Towards the end of the week, Trish came to see me. She brought along her young sister. The young sister was annoying. She giggled at everything. Drawing Mrs Dunne's attention. Mrs Dunne was always trying to get into conversations. But I was determined not to let her into this one. I wanted to find out what Colette had been doing during the holidays. She said that she would visit me, but I was afraid that she mightn't.

'She's been driving around in a bread van for the whole of the holidays,' the young sister said and shrieked with laughter. Trish nudged her hard but the little girl just nudged her back and continued, spilling the words into my worried face.

'She passed us on Knockbrack bridge and she blew the horn and shouted "Fuck the nuns".' Trish's sister was talking too loud. I didn't want Mrs Dunne to hear what she was saying. My face was falling. I could feel it. I knew Mrs Dunne would see it. I didn't want her to know the reason. 'There was a man with an earring in the passenger seat.'

Trish shouted at her sister, 'Keep your voice down!' but that only made Mrs Dunne stare even more.

'She told us to tell you she sent her love.'

'She must be busy then.'

'She's been in that van the whole time.'

I didn't speak. Colette was having a great time. She wouldn't come to see me. I knew it. I couldn't even drive. I had never seen a man with an earring. I lay very still. My body felt like glass. It didn't seem worth starving myself now, but when my supper arrived I didn't feel like it anyway. I told Trish to take the sausages and rashers as I would only eat the egg and tomatoes.

'I don't know where you get the willpower,' Trish said, squeezing the sausage between her grimy fingers.

Mrs Dunne watched them eat my food and her eyes narrowed.

She must have had a word with Matron or something, because next morning when they were doing the rounds Matron nearly took the face off me. Or they might have seen the chicken breasts in the bin. Anyway, Matron had been really nice to me all along.

Patting my head. Saying that I was the youngest girl on her floor. And that I had lovely hair.

The next thing she was gone berserk. She came flying into the room, wrenched back the covers and told me to sit up for my blood pressure. I couldn't speak or defend myself, because I'd the thermometer in my mouth. She pumped up the sphygmomanometer like mad, I thought that my arm was going to burst.

'No appreciation whatsoever. There's people who would give their two eyes to get the food you get here! But no! You have to throw it out! Give it away! What in Moses' name do you think you're playing at!'

Her white-clothed chest was rising and falling so fast, I was afraid for her. I couldn't explain. She wouldn't understand.

'Just wait till Dr Burke sees you. He's going to be furious. After all the trouble he has gone to. And your poor mother.' Matron snapped out on her black medium heels, muttering, 'Wilful waste!' as she went.

I didn't think that Dr Burke would be mad. He was always very nice. Small. With a dicky bow. He wouldn't say anything.

He did. He went mad. Tried to frighten me.

'Right,' he said and his lips went really thin. 'Do you want to die?'

'No.'

'Oh *good.* Well then, let me tell you something. If you go on the way you're going you *will* die.'

Mrs Dunne nearly fell out of her bed. Matron noticed her and drew the curtains. As if she wouldn't be able to hear anyway.

He was frightening the hell out of me. Not because I thought I was going to die, but because I thought that he was going to attack me any minute. A vein started going on his forehead. I burst out crying.

'Good. Have I frightened you?'

'Yes.'

'Good.'

'Do you know that you're halfway on the road to anorexia?' He was really exaggerating.

I began to sob harder. It was awful that he thought I had anorexia when I wasn't even quarter of the way there. Now I'd never get really thin, because they would be all watching me.

'When I think of all the work I do! And you just laughing at me. Destroying everything.'

He was gone completely mad. I cried harder.

Matron put her hand on his arm. 'That's enough, now. I'm sure she's learnt her lesson. Do you want me to leave the curtains for a while?'

'Yes.'

He walked out and gave me a really hurt look as he went. His bow tie was crooked.

Matron said, 'Think of the starving in Africa.' And followed him with stiff steps.

· *Twenty* ·

The results of all the tests were negative, so Burke said I would have to come back with my next abscess so that they could take a culture. From the culture they would manufacture a vaccine and I would become immune to the infection. It was all scientific, with everything fitting into an orderly plan. With science there was only one right answer. As Delia said. I just had to wait until I got another abscess.

But I didn't get any more abscesses while I was at home. I seemed to get abscesses only when I was at Mayo. I wondered if it was something to do with the food. At home I ate more fresh fruit and vegetables. At Mayo the vegetables were inedible and we hardly ever got fruit. Just a banana every now and then for breakfast.

Except for the leaving certs. If they became Children of Mary they always got bananas. There was one leaving cert from Dublin who'd refused to become a Child of Mary and she never got a banana for breakfast. Colm gave her table a sour look every morning.

I hated meat, it revolted me, the smell and the texture. I thought of the greasy shards we got in school. It was not just because it was cruel to animals to eat meat that I disliked it. There was a horrible feel of eating flesh, sinew and muscle. When I looked at kidneys, I thought of the nephrons that collected the waste. Each nephron had a bowmans capsule, with little threads of blood in it. It was horrible, imagine putting a bowman's capsule in your mouth and crunching it. I thought of how the little threads would get between my teeth. The whole thing of eating meat was being part of nature. Savage. Disgusting. Eating a chicken thigh was no different from a lion tearing a haunch of a deer. This was linked with growing into a woman. And having babies. Being all fleshy and savage. And men shooting animals and eating them. I saw a skinned rabbit once in a butcher's shop. It was like a little cat. I cried every time I thought about it. For about a week.

I wanted to be outside of it all. I wished that I could leave school and go and live with Colette somewhere. We could live on yogurt and smoke all the time. Smoke Marlboro.

The night I came back, I couldn't wait to tell the other girls and especially Colette about the tests I'd had in hospital and how the Matron thought that I had anorexia.

'They took a swab from my nose and honestly it was like a red-hot poker through my brain and they took so much blood in these huge syringes, I couldn't lift my head off the pillow for six hours afterwards.'

Trish said, 'Jesus wept!'

Colette laughed and threw her eyes upwards, but I was so pleased to see her that I didn't care. She rolled the curtains around her waist and stood attached to the rails, drawing attention to her waist.

But Trish and Colette had been to dances. Trish had a boyfriend and not only that, he was fashionable. He wore a grandfather shirt and braces. I didn't like it. But I preferred Colette to any boy no matter what he wore. Except Johnny. And he was a kind of dream figure.

'Johnny's going to come down and see us.'

'Oh no.'

'What's wrong with you? You don't have to meet him if you don't want to.'

'Why would I want to meet him?'

Colette started humming and running up and down past my bed, holding on to the curtains.

'You'll break them.'

'I don't care! I don't care! I'm in love!'

My stomach churned, it was hardly me she was talking about. I'd been waiting for it, but I wasn't ready. I didn't ask questions. It was no good. It was coming anyway, no matter what I did.

Colette said she had been having a secret affair with a bread-van driver. She said he was a brilliant lover and he wore an earring. I stared at her hard and decided she was making it up. She just wanted to seem normal in front of Trish and I supposed that was okay. I was more mature. I didn't need to pretend that I had boyfriends.

But when Colette came to bed, she only wanted to talk about the bread-van driver. She scarcely touched me except to pinch my arm lightly when she thought my attention was wandering. She said he was really an artist but he drove the van to live. He was going to come to see her. Under the cover of delivering bread to the convent.

'And will the nuns want it? Won't they know he's not the usual bread man?'

'He'll bluff his way in, don't worry,' Colette said. 'He's very persuasive.'

As if it was something to be proud of, as if to be

persuaded by some filthy horrible boyfriend was something great. I wanted to cry.

'Are you not afraid of . . .' I began and then stopped. Serve her right if she got pregnant. I wouldn't warn her.

'Am I afraid he'll find another mistress? I'm terrified. He's so good-looking every woman wants him, that's why I'll have to see him during the term. How will we manage it?'

'What do you mean how will *we* manage it, I'm not doing anything!'

'But you must meet him and he's an artist and everything.'

'Look, I don't want to meet him and I hate men. I've a load of study to do for the summer exams.'

'He will have lots of cigarettes,' Colette said.

I wavered, thinking that perhaps I would go, at least to get an idea of what was going on. I knew I was ignorant and I needed to know things. But the thought sickened me. 'No, I can't and that's final.'

Colette stayed on, long after the lights went out. She talked about her boyfriend all the time and how she missed his embrace. She actually said the word *embrace.*

'Once you've had it,' she said and then shook her head. I watched the grey curtains waver in the breeze she was creating, pacing, giggling, talking about Noel, Noel, Noel. She didn't even touch me and I was dying for the cool pressure of her hands.

'We'll still be friends, babe,' she said, brushing her lips across my forehead before she stole back to Saint Joseph's.

· *Twenty-one* ·

I started reading novels again. Even in class. I'd studied so hard the term before, the teachers didn't notice me drifting away. Maths had gone from algebra to geometry and geometry was pencil-chewing stuff. It was so pencil-chewing and thoughtful, I couldn't keep my mind on it.

I was breathing the clean air of hunger. I chewed orange skins. Colette was dieting too, but she was studying as well. I half-heartedly tried to avoid her but I couldn't seem to manage it.

I waited for the bread-van driver to be involved in a really bad accident.

I watched Trish become addicted to geometry. I became jealous of geometry too. Trish could spend all evening looking at triangles, arcs and circles and debating 'if this angle is equal to the sum of these two angles, then that line bisects . . .'

I waited for an abscess.

Then one Sunday morning at Mass, I was leaning my chin on my hands when I noticed that it felt slightly tender. I always felt good on Sunday mornings with the hymn singing and Benediction and incense flying through the air. With my hair freshly washed and my white shirt just laundered, I felt clean and good. I fingered my bottle-green tie and slid my hand behind the belt of my Sunday uniform which had become so pleasantly loose. Father Hognett came out with the golden monstrance which held a little white host in the middle. He held it high and my spirits rose as I felt my chin once more and thought *I have an abscess*!

I walked slowly through the cloister with Trish, testing and pressing my chin. I thought that I'd better check the mirror first, before I broke the news of abscess number twenty-five.

We went upstairs to the dormitory to put away our blazers and I rushed to the looking glass. My chin looked shiny and red in the glass. I was sure. After breakfast, I went to Carmel. 'I've got another abscess, Sister.'

Carmel looked sympathetic. Like a kitten.

'Is it a sex kitten, you mean?' Colette asked, when I described her afterwards.

'I'll tell Sister Paul this instant.' Sister Carmel looked so serious, I felt a quiver of fear. Maybe I was wrong and it wasn't an abscess.

Paul sent a message by Colm who told me that I was to leave at the soonest possibility, as if I had scarlet fever or something even worse. Carmel had the keys to Paul's office and we rang my mother from there. Carmel's little tufts of feet didn't even touch the floor when she sat in Philomena's chair to make the call.

At half past eleven, I ate a ham sandwich on my own in the refectory. Sister Carmel stood beside the table. She had made a huge pot of black coffee and she blushed as she put it on the table. I think she thought that we were living dangerously.

My mother drove me away from the convent in a rush. As if she was to blame or something. I sat hunched up in the front seat of the car, tickling my chin with the sleeve of my wool blazer.

'What in the name of God is that terrible smell?' my mother cried out suddenly.

'What smell?'

'A terrible fishy smell, is it you?'

'That's a horrible thing to say. I can't smell anything. Maybe it's yourself.'

'Don't be so cheeky. No, there is a terrible smell. It's coming from the back seat.'

I looked round and saw the brown paper parcel that Trish had put on the back seat. Months of doses of cod liver oil, secreted in coffee jars. Trish had decided that it was time to get rid of it and I'd forgotten that she had put it in.

'It's my tonic!'

'Your what?' said my mother and the car swerved as she looked back.

She could not be persuaded to carry the smell any further.

'You must be joking,' she said, darting the car down a small country road. The road grew narrower and narrower. A thick soft ruff of grass sprang down the middle. It did not look well travelled.

'Do you think it's private?' I worried.

'Give me the parcel,' my mother held out her hand.

'What if someone sees you?'

'They won't. Now stop that nonsense. Hand over that parcel.'

I handed it over slowly, noticing as I did that the cod liver oil with added malt was seeping through the paper. My mother grabbed it impatiently and the bag tore. The little 2oz coffee jars plopped one by one onto the damp grass.

'Mother of Divine Jesus!' my mother screamed, running to the car, pulling fistfuls of Kleenex from the glove compartment. She ran back and with her hands wrapped in tissue began throwing the coffee jars over the ditch.

She stood on the ditch, with one knee bent, her thin hip thrown out. She flung wildly. Her black hair came down from its bun and whizzed behind her in the wind like a banner. As she hurled the jars, her face savage, I saw a tiny figure in the background. The figure grew bigger as it approached and I could make out a tall white-haired man carrying a pitchfork.

'Mummy, there's a man!'

'Hah!' shrieked my mother as she threw the last coffee jar over the ditch and half fell, half slid down the side of the damp grassy bank.

We ran to the car and my mother turned the key frantically, the door of the driver seat wide open. The car roared awake and my mother turned an arc, just skimming a big stone that lay beside the ditch.

'Your door,' I screamed and as she banged it shut, I could hear the man say, 'Hi, hi! Shtop!' his cross face struggling over the other side of the ditch.

My mother was delighted when we got away, 'Well I'll never forget that man's face!' she said again, as she drove triumphantly away from the scene of her crime. 'I suppose he'll be talking about it for the next ten years.'

I was embarrassed, but I had to say something. 'Wasn't it . . .' I couldn't go on when she looked at me with that mad face. Her bun quivering.

'Wasn't it what?' she demanded and her eyes drifted to my chin.

I covered my chin with my hand. 'What about litter louts?' I said foolishly.

'What about them?' she said crossly and parked the car.

'Don't talk to *me* about litter louts,' she said then after a while. As if she suffered from them. 'I'll tell you something else. That's a pimple you've got on your chin.'

When we got inside, she went on and on about her homemade soup, 'There's isn't a morsel of fat in that, not that much,' she flicked her finger, 'I skimmed and I skimmed and then I left it overnight and a plate of fat had formed on the surface. I gave it to the birds. It will keep them warm.'

She was doing it all for my benefit, but it was only driving me mad. I didn't want to think about fat being near the soup. At any time, whether it was in the past or not. Why did she have to talk about fat all the time?

I looked out the kitchen window. The gigantic plate of fat dwarfed the bird table. A lonely looking sparrow walked around it, picking his way with skinny legs. He didn't seem to recognise it as food.

After dinner, we walked for ages down by the river. Long after sunset and the trees were dark patches that moved this way and that, covering and uncovering the crumbly moon. It would have been perfect if my mother hadn't mentioned Delia.

'Delia is so good. You know she's written to me three times from Dublin in the last week?'

'Really?'

'Oh, yes, "I miss you so much Auntie Eileen," ' mother quoted. 'She says she can't study with the loneliness.'

'She always says that, says she's going to fail and then comes out with honours.'

'Electrical engineering is no joke.'

'Well, she must be as good as the rest of them, didn't she get the maximum number of points in the leaving cert according to Auntie Catherine? More than anyone ever got before or could hope to get again.'

'Don't be so sarcastic, Grace. Jealousy doesn't suit you.'

'I'm not jealous. I don't want everyone to love me.'

'We'll say no more,' my mother said firmly in her appalled voice. As if she just couldn't fathom my jealousy. I knew she was making up her own mind and she'd never listen to me anyway. I thought she was lost and pathetic, trying to be Delia's special friend all the time. I touched her thin wrist. 'Let's go back by the fields.'

The wet grass brushed against our long coats and my mother threw back her head to the night air.

'This air is great for the eyes. It makes them sparkle. My mother never put anything apart from rainwater on her face.'

'And was it good?'

'Good? There will never be a complexion like it again.'

'Did you like her?'

'Like her? What a strange question to ask me. Everyone likes their mother. That's if they're natural.' She hesitated and gave me a queer look. Dark patterns of leaves moved across her face.

'And I like you,' I said. I meant it too. Even though she broke my heart. Making me jealous of Delia.

'Well, that's a relief,' she said and she sounded as young as anything.

I put my hand up the sleeve of her tweed coat and caught hold of her wrist. She turned her hand around to hold mine even though it was a bit awkward and I was afraid she'd get embarrassed.

The trees around our house darkened around us, and our feet slipped unsurely on the wet grass. As we came up through the last field, the light from the back door lit up our path and we walked to the fence at the bottom of our garden. We stopped in the field behind the house.

'Isn't it strange?' my mother said. 'I've never seen it like this, and look at the backyard light shining against the wall.'

We delayed outside, looking at the back of the house with our heads held to one side. I was imagining Delia being killed in the accident with the bread-van driver.

'I was afraid of her, too,' my mother said.

'Who?' I asked, delighted for half a second.

'My mother of course, she didn't mind making a show of you in front of anyone.' My mother sounded half guilty as she pushed in the back door. I knew what she was thinking. *God forgive me for speaking ill of the dead.*

In the kitchen, she laughed in an over relaxed way. At nothing. Twirling the belt of her grey coat. I began to worry that maybe she was going mad. I thought about the way she'd thrown away all the cod liver oil jars.

I took out a book and started reading.

But I was sorry later that I hadn't asked her more about her mother. I stood outside her bedroom when we were going to bed. I wanted to sleep with her but I was too shy to ask.

Imagine being shy of your own mother!

'Well, good night,' she said cheerfully and slammed her bedroom door. The long curtains at the window of the landing lifted slightly in the draught.

When I got inside my own door, I locked it in a sudden panic. As if the devil was already breathing outside the door, his big red hands ready to push the door in. Reading *The Exorcist* was like taking acid. You kept getting flashbacks. When you least expected them.

I knew all about LSD. I had read *Go Ask Alice.*

My mother's radio came on and Strauss waltzes tripped across the corridor to my room. As I drifted into sleep, my head muffled under the blankets, I remembered how I'd danced the *Blue Danube* with Colette at the beginning of the year.

I woke up the next morning to the pips as Radio Eireann came on the air. First it was the 'dong, dong, dong' of O'Donnell Abu, the signature tune, and then the sea forecasts, 'light decreasing to moderate, Malin Head, South East, nine knots, five miles, a thousand and ten millibars, falling slowly . . . Rosslare, East South-East . . . mist . . . Valentia. . . . Belmullet. . . . East South-East. . . . Carlingford Loch.'

Mysterious coastal stations waking up to information. Sensible people wearing Aran jumpers and being scientific. I wished that I really had an abscess and not just a pimple on my chin.

· Twenty-two ·

I didn't go to hospital because I had to admit it was only a pimple after all. My mother said she'd thought so all the time but she didn't want to say. But she didn't tell the nuns and she was nonchalant to Paul about it, saying that Burke the consultant had the matter in hand. I was beginning to feel really warm towards her in the hotel where we stopped for tea on the way back to Mayo. But then she started crying, 'Oh, why can't you always be nice to me!'

I could have said exactly the same thing, but I didn't. I thought that she must have had too much sherry.

When I got back to the dormitory, Colette arrived and sat down on my bed.

'Where were you, you weren't in study?' I asked.

'Oh, I didn't bother, I was too depressed. Was I missed?'

'No,' I said joyfully, as mad hope rose in my chest. Was it all off with the bread-van driver?

I waited expectantly and Colette announced, 'The plans are laid!'

'What plans?' I said, looking at Colette's jaw and thinking how sharp and thin it had become. Sometimes her head just looked like a skull with skin stretched over it. Lovely.

'We're going to go down town to confession, and meet him in the Rebel Bar at lunchtime, he's going to bring a friend.'

'I thought he was going to deliver bread to the convent,' I said dully.

'He got the sack from that job. Noel is too independent anyway and he needs time to concentrate on his painting. The only problem is, he has to hitch down from Cork.'

I was dubious, but at least I could get in some drinking practice. 'I hope that his friend isn't meant for me, you know I hate men.'

I agreed to go in the end. When Colette promised to ring Noel and cancel the friend. Saturday morning we got ready. Colette had got a loan of flowery 'peasant-style' dresses from Noreen O'Donovan. They were both blue, mine was a kind of sky blue and Colette's was pale powder blue. Colette's had about an inch of lace underneath.

'Will I tear off the lace?' Colette said, bunching the frothy lace in her fist.

'Don't for God's sake,' I said, my nerves jangling.

'The Rebel Bar will think that the Legion of Mary have arrived,' Colette said, looking at her reflection in the mirror.

She tried to look pious but her Spock eyebrows were all wrong and we started laughing. We had to lie down on the bed to get rid of all the laughing. It was spreading inside us like a pain. When we were finished, we turned our backs to each other, putting on our knee-high bottle-green socks. We didn't dare look at each other in case the mad laughter came back again. Then we put our bottle-green gabardine coats over our dresses. We belted them tightly, pulling the belt to the last because we both had grown very thin.

Colette's lace was hanging underneath. 'Jesus I'll fucking cut it,' she said.

'Don't!' I almost screamed with the tension, and I pinned it up with a safety pin, tearing the lace in my hurry.

We put on our green berets as well. We looked really weird. At least Colette did. I thought that I just looked like someone about to go cutting turf. In a postcard of the Real Ireland.

'You're like someone from the IRA,' I said. 'All you need is the dark glasses.'

'Good thinking, Volunteer Jones. Now, where are my sunglasses?'

She took ages. Pulling out the trunk from under her bed and rifling through old duffle bags. Rooting through all her drawers. Finally, she found a pair in the top pocket of her blazer.

'When were you wearing those with your blazer?'

'I sometimes wear them at Mass.'

'Never!'

'I'm only kidding.'

I was kind of disappointed. It was a funny idea, wearing sunglasses to Mass.

'Sorry, I can't give you a pair, comrade. But I've only got these ones.'

'I thought that I was supposed to be a volunteer. Comrades are communists aren't they?'

'You want to be a volunteer, do you?'

'I don't really. I think it's a stupid idea. We're supposed to be in disguise, not attracting the Special Branch.'

'Special Branch? Do you think there's a Special Branch in Mayo. A fart of a town? You must be joking.'

I persuaded her to take off the glasses. I thought that they were unlucky.

But, when we got to the Rebel Bar, the barman said, 'Ye forgot the Armalite rifles, girls.'

Noel was there. It was really embarrassing. Everybody was laughing at us. Even I could see that Noel was just lovely. His black curly hair was cut in the shape of an eskimo's hat. His hands were small, brown and a little bent at the knuckles. They looked very clean. I watched them rubbing Colette's back as she threw herself in for the passionate embrace. They were exactly the same height. I felt jealousy rising in my chest again and I began to examine the cigarette machine. Casually. They didn't have Marlboro.

'Give us a cigarette, quick, I'm dying for one.' Colette threw her head back as if she was in an ad for Carling Black Label or something.

'Are you dying as well?' Noel asked me.

'I've had a terrible craving for nicotine all morning,' I admitted.

'I was expelled from Collaiste Mhuire for smoking,' Noel said.

'That's awful.'

'I was delighted. I thought they never would,' Noel answered. Thrilling me.

'They starved us,' he said and pointed to a bulging plastic bag. 'Look.' He delved his little brown hands into the bag. 'Honeycrisp, Mars Bars, Catches, Crunchies, Pub Taytos.'

'For fuck's sake, Noel. There was no need.' Colette pulled at the bag with her purple fingers. I knew she was thinking about our diets. It was torture.

Noel lifted more packets. 'Scots Clan, Emerald, Yorkies. Rum and Butter. Tuc Biscuits.'

'Three Counties Cheese,' said Colette despairingly.

Spreadable cheese was out. A year's calories in one triangle.

'You need fattening,' Noel said, patting her bottom.

I looked away. Mortified.

'I'll have a Power's whisky,' said Colette.

'With what?' said Noel.

'Nothing, I'm drinking it straight.'

I didn't think she'd be able for whisky in any form. We had nothing in our stomachs. I asked for a vodka and orange anyway. The drink hit my stomach in a vicious attack. I could see that Colette was trying not to shudder and I went up to get peanuts. She didn't try to stop me.

There was a fat man standing at the bar, holding a pint of Guinness. 'Any chance you'd come to the Lilac for a dance tonight?' he smirked at me.

The skin on my scalp lifted when I saw the way he looked at me. 'How dare you speak to me,' I said.

'A cat may look at a queen,' he said, leering with confidence.

'Shut up, yourself.' I was really savage.

'Ah, you're nothing but a frigid Brigid,' the man said and then maliciously, 'do the nuns know you're out?'

'You must be thirty if you're a day!' I picked up the peanuts and left the bar, swishing my peasant-style dress as I went. I sat down at our table and stared back at the man. I'd stare him out if it killed me. But he had all day. He folded his arms. Delighted with himself. I thought I would cry. What right had he to look at me like that? It made me sick.

'Don't take any notice,' Noel said, putting his arm round me. Colette looked at Noel's arm and the man turned back to the counter. 'You must ignore people like that.'

'But he's got no right.'

'Have another cigarette.' Noel winked at me. 'Sure, he's pathetic.'

I looked back at the man and saw what Noel meant. Now Noel would think I was horrible. And I wasn't really. Noel tried to stop me but I was gone.

I bought another packet of peanuts and I smiled at the fat man.

I turned away quickly, feeling embarrassed. It was a hard thing to do. I headed for the table, relieved. Then, I got stuck behind a man carrying four pints and I thought I felt a slight pinch on my bottom. I couldn't believe it and I turned round. There was the fat man. Leering again.

I punched him in the stomach. I kicked him in the ankles twice. Silence fell in the crowded bar.

'Jaysus, she's a bloody lunatic,' I heard someone mutter.

I hated men. They were dirty pigs. The fat man was laughing and I was crying. Colette gathered our coats, Noel took my arm.

'We're going to O'Brien's next door,' they said and dragged me with them.

The bar man came after us with the plastic bag of sweets.

I sat in a corner of O'Brien's, feeling disgraced. Noel and Colette tried to cheer me up.

'He's only a moron,' Colette said.

'You've got to learn to ignore those types completely. No point in being nice and there's no point in getting into a fight.'

'I didn't get into a fight.'

'I know you didn't.' Noel gave my arm a squeeze. 'Make Love not War.' He started laughing.

'Fuck off, you old fool.' Colette lit another cigarette.

Noel bought me a double vodka. I lit cigarette after cigarette and blew the smoke out vehemently.

'It's not myself I'm worried about,' I said. 'It's all women. I'm a feminist.'

'So am I,' said Noel. And I was glad he didn't ask me about it.

The more I drank, the stronger and tougher I felt. I felt I was going to have a revelation, but I forgot what I was going to say. I sat and smiled at Noel and Colette. Colette looked very happy too. She was holding hands with Noel. I knew that I was having a great time.

I leaned forward to say something but I became queasy. For no reason. I felt strange. I felt pale. The revelatory feeling left me. I was dizzy. I sat very still but it didn't help. I wondered if it was a brain haemorrhage. Then I felt sick and rushed to the Ladies' room through a set of saloon-type doors that banged and flapped behind me like I was Jesse James. I bent over the toilet, retching, the vodka burning up through my throat.

The long flowing sleeves of my Legion of Mary dress kept getting in the way. What would we say to Noreen O'Donovan, I wondered, standing up, breathless. But I had no time to think as another wave of sickness plunged over me and I bent over the toilet again. I heard Colette coming in.

'Is that you, Colette?' I called.

I couldn't understand what she was saying, but at least she was coming in to help me. Her footsteps went past and I heard her vomiting in the toilet next door.

When we came out of the toilets, we shivered and pushed up the sleeves of our blue dresses. There was no hot water and no soap. We had to use cold water. Colette said it was good for us and splashed loads of freezing water on our faces, necks and arms.

We were purple and freezing. Looking stupid when we joined Noel at the table. He had two glasses of

Tanora ready for us. I was glad he hadn't brought his friend with him. I didn't mind Noel so much, he seemed to take it all in his stride. He was twenty-one and very mature. He had spent a year in London as well, living in a squat, and painting on the pavements. He told us about the freedom and the other artists. He said he would go back to London because he couldn't 'stick the narrowminded Irish mentality'. He quoted Joyce, '*We are an unfortunate priestridden race, and always were and always will be, till the end of the chapter.*'

'That's lovely,' I said. 'Did he say anything about nuns?'

We were eating a big bar of Dairy Milk chocolate that Noel had taken out of the plastic bag. We had gone past dieting. I thought it would be nice if there were places one could go to drink Tanora and eat chocolate and talk about books instead of having to drink vodka in cold bars where horrible men lurked gawping over their pints.

The door of the bar opened, and two hippies came in. They came straight over to Noel. One of them was Johnny.

'What are you doing to my sister? She's drinking Tanora.'

'Oh, she's got a bad stomach.'

'Not at all. Colette's stomach is made of iron.' Johnny slapped her on the back and looked at me. I put my hand up to my hair. I hated the way I was looking. Johnny had his hair tied back with a navy velvet ribbon. His eyes were navy too.

The other man had round gold-rimmed glasses and he spoke with an English accent.

'I like your dresses,' Johnny said to Colette, his mouth turning up at the corners. He looked so cynical. Like that lord out of *The Picture of Dorian Grey.*

'They're awful,' I said.

'Ah, they're cute,' he said and stared at me. 'Are you going to roll up, Davy?' he asked and kept staring at me. Colette gave him a really mad look then and he snapped his eyes away. It was a relief. But I hoped that he would look back at me. He didn't. He was staring at Davy's hands.

The hippy took out a tobacco pouch and tiny little flimsy squares of white paper that came in a red packet. With Rizla written on it. He licked his fingers and started rolling up tobacco in the paper. I had never seen anyone making cigarettes before. It looked really hard.

Noel looked keen. 'Have you got any gear?' he said tightly, as if he had been winded.

Davy looked gently through his gold-rimmed glasses. 'I've got some really good stuff, man. A present from Tim Daly, all the way from Kilcrohane, man.'

They were like terriers, pricking up their ears and sniffing at the clear plastic bag of greeny brown mud that Davy took out of the pocket of his flowery waistcoat.

I leaned forward as well.

And then for no reason, Colette jumped up and picked up her gaberdine coat. 'God, look at the time. We'll be missed. Come on, Grace.' She picked up my coat and before I knew where I was she was putting my arms into the sleeves of my gaberdine coat. I didn't want to go, but I couldn't say anything. I saw Colette exchanging looks with Johnny.

It was a jolt when I remembered Mayo. It seemed like years since I'd been there. I wanted to see what happened when they opened the bag of green mud.

'Look at the time!' Colette said. And we had to go. I belted my coat and tucked my hair behind my ears. I wanted to look unconcerned. I wanted to look at

Johnny but resisted. I examined a scuff mark on my shoe.

When Colette said goodbye, she clung to Noel. I went red but he didn't mind, he kissed her back. There were shy country types up at the bar and they turned their backs after goggling for about a minute. I turned away.

'Will I kiss you?' Johnny asked.

'No,' I said and then felt stupid.

When we were putting on our berets and hiding the cigarettes down our socks, he whispered, 'Haven't the nuns told you about free love?'

'I love only Colette,' I said. Trying to be aloof.

'I know,' he said and smiled. 'Colette told me all about you.'

I looked at his crooked tooth and wondered what Colette had told him. In a rush of confusion I went out the door before Colette had finished kissing Noel.

Outside on the pavement, I felt stupid. People stared at me, I hoped they weren't going to report me. I looked in a window, trying to be casual. People stared even more. I read the sign on the window, *Double Diamond Works Wonders.* I felt sick thinking about what Colette might have said to Johnny.

'Did you say anything to Johnny about me?' I asked Colette as we pelted, breathless, up the convent avenue.

'How do you mean?'

'Well, did you tell him about us?'

'Of course I told him about us. Didn't he see us together in the pub?'

'No, but did you tell him about us in bed.'

'Oh, I did. He loves hearing about it. I told him that we went all the way.'

'No!'

'He understands, he's very broad-minded.'

'No, Colette. You couldn't have! Please, please, tell me you didn't.'

'All right so, I didn't.'

'I don't believe you.' My face was burning with shame.

'And I told him how you were always asking questions about him. Like about his clothes and everything.'

'I can't bear it,' I said when we got to the cloister door.

'Don't be so stupid.'

'I don't care, I don't care. I'm going to drown myself.' I ran towards the walks, heading for the stream.

'Don't be such an eedjit.'

'I can't go on.'

'Shut up.'

I ran ahead of Colette. She pelted after me, pulling at my gaberdine. When I got to the stream, I stopped. It looked so cold. But I took off my shoes and socks anyway, holding onto the branch of a tree for support.

'What are you doing?' Colette asked. Stupidly, I thought.

'Getting prepared.'

'But you need your clothes if you want to drown. You need them to drag you down.'

'Shut up! Nothing will stop me now.'

'Oh don't be so stupid. You couldn't drown a cat in that stream. I didn't tell Johnny anyway. I just couldn't resist saying it. You should have seen your face.'

'Really?'

'Yes, really. Come on back. We'll get caught.'

'But you mean it, Colette?'

'I do.'

'Because I would never talk to you again.'

'What do you think I am anyway? Why would I tell him? I wouldn't want him to know about what we did.'

I did believe her then. We decided to cut through the trees. Out feet sank in the wet marshy ground and our long dresses sank in the mud. I was thinking about Johnny. About his Levis. Not as faded as his other pair. His navy-blue ribbon, his navy-blue eyes. The way he looked at me.

· *Twenty-three* ·

Noel went back to London soon after that. Colette said that she thought that her heart would break, but she was studying very hard. Besides I refused to show any interest in Colette's broken heart. I'd enough to do, contending with my own heart, and all the jealousy Colette had brought upon me.

We hadn't got any thinner, because every now and then we felt so weak that we had to eat a load of chocolate. I was the only one who wasn't studying, Trish and Colette were eating the books. I spent a lot of time trying to read James Joyce. I had brought *Portrait of the Artist as a Young Man* in the local bookshop. I couldn't understand it. It spoke about things like wetting the bed, things that nobody wanted to remember.

Before the mid-term break, I got a real abscess under my arm. I went to the laboratory in the hospital. A nun whose eyes were at the level of my armpit took the sample, wielding a very long needle. I wondered did she get that job because she was so small.

As the weeks went by, I daydreamed and doodled. Sometimes I worked out Pythagoras's theorem, pretending to myself that I was Pythagoras and was in the process of deducing it for the first time.

'Eureka,' I liked to say to myself as I wrote QED, even though it had been Archimedes who had said that. I liked that word a lot, although it was embarrassing to think of Archimedes who ran from his bath naked through the streets, according to Colette.

'You wouldn't think it embarrassing if he was young and dishy.'

'He was bound to be old and have a beard. I'd say he had white hair.'

'You're thinking of God the Father.'

After two weeks there was still no vaccine. It had got lost in the post. Sister Paul called me into the office and told me that I would have to get another abscess as the hospital seemed to have mislaid the rest of the sample.

'You must be brave now, Grace. Everybody is doing their best, you know.'

I gulped with disappointment and slunk out of the office. She wasn't the one who had to get another abscess if they had lost the vaccine. Why did she always have to shout so loud? And those eyes. Joining up, like Balor the Fomorian. She gave me a headache.

I went back to the study dejectedly. There was a skittering sound when I came in. Loads of girls turned around. To look. It wasn't often that girls got called to Paul's office. And it was always for serious things. Like getting expelled or your relatives dying.

Trish turned round. 'What did she want?'

'They lost my vaccine,' I whispered as low as I possibly could. Everybody was looking at me, I couldn't bear to give them any information.

'Oh God, that's desperate!'

'I know.' I stared back at Noreen O'Donovan who was staring across at me. She looked away.

Suddenly I was crying. I was amazed that it should happen to me, but I could hear a terrible noise like a banshee's wail coming from my throat. I tried to stop but it only got worse.

Mother Colm got down off her high chair, 'Will you stop that acting, Grace Jones! Is there no limit that you won't go to to look for notice? People have been bending themselves over backwards to get you your vaccine and all you can do is start this caterwauling. Have you no respect for the other girls? Some people have to study you know, they haven't been blessed with your brains.'

'She's very upset, Sister,' Trish said.

I cried harder.

I could hear Colm's voice from a long distance away saying, 'Stop that silly crying and pull yourself together this instant!'

But now I was weeping soundlessly in shame for what had happened to me in front of everyone.

'Take her up to the dormitory, she's trying to cause a scene and upset the whole study!'

Trish took my arm and led me out. The door slipped out of her hand when she was leaving and banged like mad. The glass panels shivered.

In the dormitory, I got under my bedclothes with my clothes on and wept again. Trish handed me tissues from a box. I wanted to speak but as fast as I wiped, the tears came back. And my shoulders were shaking and everything.

After a few minutes, we heard soft padding and the scrape of Sister Carmel's housecoat as she rushed into the dormitory, 'Grace, you poor creature! What happened?'

'Mother Colm thinks I'm trying to cause trouble,' I wailed, loud again.

'Now, now, she doesn't. Where did you get that idea?'

'She told me herself, below in the study. Didn't she Trish?'

Sister Carmel turned to Trish, 'There's a tray outside on Saint Anthony's table. Can you bring it in to me before you go?'

Sister Carmel had made a flask of hot coffee and she gave me three tiny white pills to take. I drank the coffee, still snuffling. And swallowed the pills. Sister Carmel reached into her pocket then and took out six chocolates wrapped in a piece of tissue.

'Now, tell me where you got this strange idea?'

I tried to explain that Mother Colm had a terrible bad opinion of me and Carmel listened. She didn't say a word. It made me want to explain even more. But I had to fight hard to talk, because my voice was slowing down. And then I was gone. Into the deepest sleep ever.

Carmel kept me in bed the following day and gave me more of the little white pills. 'Sister Paul said you must take them or you'll never get better,' she said anxiously.

I didn't go back to class before the mid-term break. Colette called in the night before we broke up.

'I've called in a hundred times and every time you were out for the count.'

'The tablets are making me sleepy.'

'Jesus, girl, they have you on drugs. You'd better watch it.'

'Listen, does everyone think I'm mad?'

'Not at all. We're all sick of the way Colm was treating you. She got a good fright and everyone was delighted. She has been very quiet since.'

'I don't know what happened to me.'

'Grace, listen to me,' Colette said sagely, 'She's

nothing only a frustrated sex maniac and she's jealous of you because she knows you'll get plenty of it when you get out of here. Noel told me that Johnny thought you were something else. He never stopped talking about you.'

'Go away.'

'I'm telling you! Colm is only cracking up at the thought of all the men you're going to have.'

I couldn't help laughing at Colette, even though I knew she was fooling me. She swung a few times on the curtain bars before she left me sinking into sleep again. Thinking about Johnny and his three pairs of Levis and his one pair of Wranglers. Colette said that he had torn the little piece of leather off the back pocket of his Wranglers. She said that they looked brilliant.

· *Twenty-four* ·

A couple of weeks later, Colette said we had to lose some serious weight. We hadn't lost anything for ages. I admitted that I had been having slices of brown bread, that I hadn't been going around dying with the hunger. We got all fired up one night when we sat up late, counting calories and doing press ups and sit ups. I couldn't wait to feel pure and empty again. Colette said if I was really serious, I would have to take up smoking. We were going to smoke real hard. Because we wanted to go to college. To smoke loads of dope. And study French and English.

'Fuck science!' I said.

'Yeah man,' said Colette. 'I'm sick of being good at maths.'

Trish looked at us.

'Seven hours' study a day.'

'Minimum!' Colette said.

We grew thinner, and it was nice even if the day dragged and all we had to eat for each meal was an orange. Colette slept without bedclothes as she figured she burnt up more calories that way. I couldn't sleep without blankets, as it was I had to wear hairy gorilla socks that my aunt had sent from America and two jumpers in bed.

Colette went mad. 'You've no backbone, you'll never get really thin if you're going to be that soft. Mollycoddling yourself.'

Colette's bones were showing, it was really brilliant. And the nuns were clamping down. Some of the leaving certs who had become very thin had left the school.

'They were models,' Colette said.

'They were like something you'd put out to frighten the crows,' Trish said.

I thought that they were fierce romantic.

Paul took to making surprise visits to the refectory to watch us eat, but it was easy to pretend to be eating. She couldn't watch one hundred and sixty girls at once. We scattered crumbs on our plates and pretended to be chewing fiercely every time she patrolled past our table.

The worst part was the continual icy coldness and the fact that I woke up very early with the hunger. Breakfast was our biggest meal and I looked forward so much to the half slice of brown bread and strong black coffee. Sometimes Colette allowed herself an egg but the smell nauseated me. So did Mother Colm's face as she delivered hard greyish eggs to the egg eaters from an old sweet tin.

I had stopped getting abscesses and we put it down to our healthy fat-free diet. We clung to the radiators whenever we could. I was never properly warm and I craved warmth more than food. There was one radiator that it was possible to squeeze behind, if you held your breath. Girls were always threading themselves in and out behind it. It was a kind of scale and if you couldn't get behind the radiator, you were too fat.

Trish pleaded with us to eat, but we remained stubborn. Trish was always pleading and I liked it. It made me feel wanted. I would lie my head on her desk while she 'fixed' my hair and gave motherly advice. I liked her smell, it was like oranges and peanuts. And I liked her hands. She had the nicest hands. You couldn't call them thin, they were slim. And they weren't white, they were cream-coloured.

One night I left early for my bath. It was cold on the stairs. Like January. Except that it was May. I was wondering would I cheat and have a warm bath. Colette believed that getting into ice-cold baths was a great way of losing weight. I was inclined to believe Colette's theories no matter how wild. Because she was so good at getting thin.

She believed in boiling hot baths to burn the fat off. She nearly killed me one night after robbing Carmel's electric kettle from her bedroom and bringing the water up to an unbelievable heat. I was sore for three hours afterwards and there were red marks on my shins for ages.

This night I decided that I didn't give a damn. I was going to have a warm bath and enjoy myself for once. When I came round the second last landing of the brass staircase, I bumped into Colette and Trish.

'My heart is still pounding,' Trish was saying as I came up.

'What is it?'

'Nothing,' Colette said, and Trish started giggling.

'There is something. I know there is.'

'We'll tell you when you get to the bathroom,' Colette said.

'Go on, go on,' Trish urged. 'I hear Paul down on the bottom corridor.'

I went up ahead of them, even though I sensed a trick. Then I stopped dead.

Saint Joseph and the Virgin Mary were standing outside Saint Joseph's dormitory and Saint Joseph was shaking his head sadly at me. His halo was vibrating in a horrible way. His face was dark and shadowed. Rotten-looking. And he held a card in his hand, I HOPE THAT YOU ARE GOING TO HAVE A COLD BATH AND OFFER IT UP FOR THE HOLY SOULS IN PURGATORY. I copped then he was a statue but I still screamed and ran back, down to where Colette and Trish were bent over double.

'Bloody great statues, aren't they?'

'They're awful, they look real!'

'I think it's because they've been taken down from the pedestals. They're about the same height as one of us.' Colette put her arm round Joseph and gave his halo another tweak. It started vibrating again. I couldn't bear to look at him.

'Look at the size of his feet. They're huge,' Trish said.

'You know what that's a sign of!' Colette started laughing.

'Come away from him. He's horrible.' I pulled at Colette's arm.

'Oh, let me please. I'll miss him when he's gone.'

'What are they doing here?'

'They're on their way to the convent,' Trish said. 'They're being moved in the morning. I got the fright of my life and Louise Burke fainted, it was very irresponsible to leave them here really. I mean Louise Burke could have had a heart attack or anything.'

'And what about me?'

'You were the first person we thought of,' Colette said cheerfully. 'We knew you'd give us a good laugh. And wait till we get Brenda. We'll see how much of an atheist she is, then.'

The only person who didn't get a fright was Brenda. I thought that was a very hopeful sign.

The rest of the evening was a series of screams and

cries and giggles, until eventually Mother Colm came and threw a sheet over the statues. She said that the lack of respect that was shown for religious images was absolutely appalling.

Colm came in and looked at me before she put the lights out.

'Do you know anything about this card?' She waved Saint Joseph's sign at me.

'No, Sister.'

'There is some kind of abuse going on. Don't think that I don't know about it, Grace Jones. You'd want to keep away from the holy water, I'll be watching.

I hadn't a clue what she was talking about. Colette thought that it might be something to do with the devil. That I was in league with him or something. Because the devil can't bear holy water. I thought that maybe Colm thought I was going to give Saint Joseph a bath.

The statues were taken away at the end of the week.

· *Twenty-five* ·

We could put our two hands inside the waistbands of our skirts. Colette put it down to our regular smoking. She had given up smoking in the cattle pen. Now we smoked in an old shed that had a hole in the roof. Trish often climbed up on the roof to look out for us. She didn't smoke but liked being on the farm. We never worried about the silent farm nuns.

'Those creatures would be afraid even to *look* at Paul!' Colette said and I agreed.

I cringed at the thought of Sister Paul blasting those gentle creatures with her tongue. 'I suppose they have to talk to her at meal times. Pass me the butter on the rectangular plate, if you please, Sister Mary Stanislaus,' I bellowed, imitating Paul and Trish nearly fell off the roof.

The lay nuns were nice. I told Colette and Trish what one of the leaving certs had told me. Lay nuns had to do all the menial tasks because they hadn't brought a dowry when they joined the convent. Colette and Trish said it was fucking awful and I felt satisfied. I liked nothing better than exposing injustices.

'I can't understand it. I mean they're supposed to believe that Jesus preferred poor people anyway and

Paul has a plastic carrier bag full of *The Dubliners* cassettes in her room. The capitalist pig!'

'It's easier for a camel to get through the eye of a needle than for a rich man to get into Heaven,' said Trish wisely.

'I wouldn't like to be getting Paul through the eye of a needle,' Colette said, stubbing out her cigarette on a stone jutting out from the wall.

We all nodded seriously. Thinking about the size of Paul.

'The bitch had the cheek to ask me what I'd had for dinner yesterday,' Colette said.

'What did you say?'

'I said that I had two chops, three potatoes and four helpings of carrots.'

'And did she believe you?' I couldn't get over the way Colette got away with things.

'She'd no bloody choice,' said Colette looking thundery.

Colette was quiet these days and she rarely joked like she used to. It was an effort for her to get around because she was so weak all the time. I wished things were like they were in the old days. Colette had got so serious, constantly studying and writing out French verbs on the back of her hand. I didn't worry any more about getting caught smoking. Things like Maupassant and how thin our arms were seemed more important.

One Sunday we were walking towards the refectory when a wild crowd of girls surged down the stairs screaming, 'Buns for tea! Buns for tea!'

We didn't get buns often now and when we did, there was even less to go round. Paul had some theory that girls needed more brown bread and butter to fatten them up.

Colette looked disgusted. 'They're like wild savages.

We'll go down to the radiator for a few minutes to let that racket die down.'

We passed the hungry mob which was spilling in the refectory door. I thought that I could hear Mother Colm's grumpy voice as I passed, and wondered why she was there. It was usually Sister Carmel who supervised tea. We walked down to the tall cream radiator at the end of the corridor and inserted our purple starved hands into spaces. Mother Colm passed. I heard her fast heels clicking as she walked quickly in her sensible shoes.

'Bloody hell,' Colette muttered and I turned.

My mouth fell open. Mother Colm's head was completely bare. She was clutching her veil to her quaking chest. She passed us quickly, heaving and looking embarrassed.

'Something must have happened in the refectory,' I watched the back of Colm's grey head, as it retreated, small and pathetic-looking.

We went down to see what it was. 'It's about time we went anyway, I'm really dying for my coffee,' I said, thinking hopelessly about duck loaf.

Colette smiled and looked superior. She did not admit to having any physical needs and liked to give the impression that she went to the refectory only because there was nothing else to do. We got our jars of coffee from our lockers and went to the corner of the refectory where Sister Carmel left the pots of hot water.

My stomach was rumbling and growling like a tormented bear. Colette looked disapproving. 'You'll have to get that thing under control,' she said severely.

I noticed that Sister Carmel seemed distracted. Colette told me to stop looking at her and to drink up my coffee. She put four teaspoons of coffee in each cup and we swallowed down the scalding liquid quickly.

We drank coffee so hot it burned. Colette said that it was good to mortify the throat. To stop it from swallowing too much. The caffeine raced into my bloodstream and I felt a bit high.

Trish ran into the refectory and almost collided with Carmel.

'Will you have a cup, Trish?' Colette said, firing several more spoons of coffee into her mug.

'No, I won't, thanks. Listen, there's been the most terrible thing. Colm came in to help Carmel and there was so much pushing and pulling for buns, her veil was pulled off. There's going to be absolute war. She's gone to get Paul.'

'What?'

'Yeah, and not only that but Father Hognett was kind of attacked.'

'*Attacked?*'

'Well, not exactly attacked, but . . . shh . . . tell you later.'

There was a loud banging on the bell. Paul had arrived, swollen with fury.

'I have never heard the likes in all my born days! Hand me that speaker, Sister Carmel.'

Carmel fumbled with a megaphone.

'Jesus, look! It's the thing they use for the May procession,' Colette whispered behind her hand. We had a terrible time trying to keep our faces straight.

'Give me the speaker,' Paul said to Carmel, really snappy. Carmel dropped it and caught it with her knee. Paul gave her a filthy look and wrenched it away from her. 'If you don't know how to handle it!'

I was raging but I knew that everyone would be on Carmel's side anyway. Paul switched on the megaphone. A screech filled the refectory. She turned it down.

'You might wonder why I'm using this equipment, but I have a very serious matter to announce.'

How could anyone be serious now? The room was heaving with giggles. I felt really sorry for the girls in the front row. Trish was in a terrible state. I thought that Colm would say something to her. Colette gave her a hankie, she put it over her nose and mouth.

Paul's voice was fierce funny. Muffled and loud at the same time. 'Father Hognett knocked to his face on the terrazza floor and Mother Colm's veil torn off! I've never seen such greed in all my life! You're like barbarians!'

Trish whispered, 'Father Hognett was taking a short cut from the convent through Saint Joseph's dormitory and . . .'

'Do I hear whispering at the back, there?' Paul turned up the megaphone. It screeched again. 'Stand out where I can see you, Patricia Cronin. The poor man's having his knee dressed in the kitchen at this very moment. Only that the man is a saint he'd have had you all arrested.'

Paul went on and on. Loud, low and then medium volume. The megaphone screeching and beeping. '. . . whose parents have sacrificed everything. Such selfish greedy girls I have never witnessed in all my years as principal of this school. But I will get to the bottom of this. I will and I'll find the ringleaders.' She turned up the volume again for the last bit.

When we put our mugs away, we could see into the kitchen, where Father Hognett was drinking a cup of tea. His foot was resting on a chair. But he didn't look too bad and he was eating a slice of duck loaf.

Everyone had to eat dry bread and water for a whole day. We didn't give a damn. Paul said there would never be buns for tea again. Colette was laughing. Two second-years were suspended. I felt bad about that although Colette said it was their own fault. They shouldn't have been eating buns in the first place. She was jubilant about the bread and water fast. 'They can't touch us. We are above food.'

But I knew that if they took away our coffee we would collapse.

In study, we wore our blazers and hunched over *Macbeth.* We learnt all the quotations really well, '*A drum, a drum, Macbeth doth come*' and '*Fair is foul and foul is fair.*'

'*Is this a dagger which I see before me, The handle toward my hand?*' That one was our favourite. '*Come let me clutch thee, I have thee not and yet I see thee still!*'

We stole knives from the refectory and ran up and down the dormitory to make our hair float out behind us. I liked the last bit best.

> *I go and it is done; the bell invites me*
> *Hear it not, Duncan, for it is a knell*
> *That summons thee to heaven or to hell.*

We practised our ghastly laughs and held our fingers to our noses to breathe in the nicotine smell. The smell was brilliant. I thought of Johnny. It was really spooky. I felt very thin.

· Twenty-six ·

It snowed in May. I thought that the world was coming to an end. We became very cold. Couldn't remember what it was like to feel warm. At night, I crept into Colette's dormitory and we slept together to keep the cold away. Sister Carmel found us a few times, when she called us for Mass, but she never said anything. When I woke it felt like I was in the arms of a skeleton.

One Saturday morning, Sister Carmel came early to the Little Flower dormitory. Her pink cheeks were puffed, swollen with concern. 'You must get up, Grace. You're going to hospital.'

I was weak and the room circled me. 'But Sister, why? I don't get abscesses any more.'

Sister Carmel began to cry. 'Colette is going with you. Can't you see what you've been doing? We're trying to get you to eat but you're deceiving us. You must go to hospital for help.'

'Sister Carmel, don't cry. I can't bear it.' I didn't have anorexia. I was just getting down to my proper weight. I just had desperate bad metabolism, it meant I had to eat nothing to look normal.

When I cried, it was like the time my vaccine didn't

come. I started to shake. 'Don't send us to hospital, we'll eat, I swear to God, Sister. Don't send us!'

Sister Carmel said it was out of her hands. Paul had rung my mother and she was coming at ten o'clock.

'I don't want you to go to hospital,' Sister Carmel said. 'You're too sensitive. I'd much rather you were here, I'd nurse you in the dormitory.'

I could not stop crying. It frightened me and I was afraid I was going to have a nervous breakdown. One of the leaving certs had a nervous breakdown and she couldn't stop crying either.

The cubicle door opened silently and Colette came in. Wearing her beret and her gaberdine coat tightly belted, like the day we had gone to the Rebel Bar.

'Are you ready, Volunteer Jones?'

'Take off the sunglasses,' Carmel said gently.

Colette took them off slowly. Giving Carmel cynical looks. She looked wasted. The beret pulled her hair back from her face. Bone with the skin stretched tightly over it. She frightened me, with her death's head and accusing look.

But it was her parents she was mad with. '*Gone to Tenerife. Having a lovely time, see you in two weeks.* It will be good enough for them when they find me in hospital when they come back.'

'Your parents are very fond of you,' Carmel said, looking fierce upset. I thought that she was going to cry again.

'They do in their arse! But do I care? Like fuck!' Colette examined the sole of her shoe. She looked up then and her face blazed with hatred. 'All my mother cares about is getting a tan. It doesn't matter where she is, if she's at home she's frying on that sunbed day and night. Do you know why I haven't got a photograph of her? Because I'd be ashamed to show you. She's got a face like a leather handbag.'

My mother arrived early. I heard her heels clipping on the dormitory tiles. I expected her to be angry and she was. Her bun was okay at the front but there were two lumps of hair falling down at the back. It looked really stupid. I could imagine her angry in front of the glass. Not able to put the hairclips in right, fury shaking her fingers.

She turned to Sister Carmel straight away. 'Look at me! A widow! Haven't I had enough to put up with? Look at the state of her.' She put her hands over her face and cried out, 'She's like something you'd dig up!'

I thought that she was putting it on. Trying to frighten me. Colette was a bit ghostly-looking, but I was fine. And a lot of it had to do with the way Colette had dressed herself, anyway.

'Why have you done it to me?' My mother stood in an imploring attitude. Like something you'd see at the foot of a cross.

Sister Carmel frowned and looked down at her little black shoes. She didn't answer my mother. My mother waited. She was awaiting for Carmel to castigate me. Say what a wonderful woman she was. That she was a widow, bringing me up on her own. That I was ungrateful.

Carmel said nothing and Colette started laughing. Low and sarcastic. 'Heh, heh, heh.' It was really creepy. It gave my mother a start and she dried up her tears pretty quickly. Carmel gave her a clean tissue and she put her arm out for my mother to hang on to.

The three of us went quietly in the end.

Trish was standing on the lower corridor and she waved to us as we passed by. Some of the girls were really staring. Colette looked at everyone with contempt. She took long steps through the dormitory, cutting a weird figure in her gaberdine and beret.

When we got to the cloister door, she put her sunglasses on.

'Do you need those things?' my mother asked.

'Yes,' Colette said and my mother said nothing more.

I could see that my mother was frightened. I was a bit afraid of Colette too. She definitely wasn't normal.

We got to the car and my mother pulled out rashly, scraping the nuns large brown station wagon. Colette sat up and took off her sunglasses. 'There's a big scratch on the nuns' car,' she said.

My mother ignored her, swinging the steering wheel wildly, tracing a large frantic arc in her rush to get away. She wasn't going to stop. She never did.

Colette put the sunglasses on again and started singing Van Morrison's 'Into The Mystic'. It was our favourite song. I touched her hand and tried to smile. I was annoyed to find that my face was wet with tears again. I hated all the crying, it was so embarrassing.

Colette stopped singing and began her creepy laughing again. Her mouth was all twisted and old looking.

My mother pointed her chin at the road ahead and tightened her lips. Colette was really frightening her. I could see by the way she struggled with the gearstick and flapped her left hand aimlessly at the glove box. As if she was looking for something, but was driving too fast to find it.

I wept and looked at the green fields with the black-and-white cows. Everything looked streamy through my tears. I tried to stop because I was afraid that if I didn't stop crying and Colette didn't stop laughing my mother would have a crash.

But the harder I tried, the more I cried. And the more I cried, the harder Colette laughed. We cried and laughed our way to Cork. My mother burst her tyre on the kerb outside the hospital and we went through the grounds, looking like lunatics. Colette, with her beret and dark glasses, going 'Heh, heh, heh'; my mother, with her bun falling down; and my face streaming with tears.

· *Twenty-seven* ·

I was in hospital for two weeks while they forced me to eat. I tried to see Colette. It was hard though. They watched me all the time. Once I ran down the corridor when one of the patients had some kind of turn. The nurses had their white backs to me. In a circle around the woman who had conked. I ran for it. I didn't even make the stairs, had to run into the toilet and get sick.

They thought that I got sick on purpose. And then they watched me even more carefully. I told them I got sick because the meals were too big. I had to sit really still to keep the food down. I asked them for smaller meals. They said that they couldn't be smaller. And exchanged looks. *God, she's in a bad state!*

I got fat. It was awful. Dragging myself out to the bathroom. Shielding my face from the mirror. I couldn't bear to see my reflection. I washed my hair every day, I felt so greasy and fatty. It hurt me bending down to rinse my hair in the bath. Bending over my voluminous stomachs. I was so heavy, I could hear my skeleton groaning for help. After every meal, my belly was a taut cylinder, ready to explode.

Sometimes I made myself look in the full-length mirror in the bathroom. Facing facts. Crying and crying, leaning my forehead against the cool tiles. When I ate, I cried more, the tears splashing into the food. Making the stupid jelly salty. It was such a pointless desert. Jelly and cream.

But I ate the food because I wanted to get out. I had to get away. Once I was out I could start again. Getting away was the most important thing.

They let me out when I was as fat as a fool. My mother gave me some money to buy books. And that was the first day that I began to feel kind of normal again. Walking up Patrick Street towards the Mercier Bookshop. The door jangled when I opened it. I looked at all the Penguins with their bright orange spines. I smelt the smell of print and paper. There was always books, no matter what, and my heart did a few bounds.

I bought a John Steinbeck for Colette. I was going to visit her. I hadn't seen her since the day we had come to the hospital. I went into a sweetshop, and bought six packets of sugar-free chewing gum and twenty Marlboro. You could get Marlboro in Cork. And French cigarettes in their funny lovely blue-and-white packets. Colette said that Johnny smoked them sometimes. I'd have bought a packet of Gitane except I was afraid that I wouldn't be able to pronounce Gitane properly.

I stood outside Roches Stores waiting for a number eight bus. I listened to the Echo boys as they advertised the *Evening Echo* in their Cork City accents. Going up and down. Talking to each other and saying 'like' and 'boy' all the time. I wished I was one of them. They were all small and thin. Their heads shaved. And they walked with their legs lifted high in their Doc Marten boots. They looked tough. And they looked soft. I wanted to sweep them away with me. Or them to sweep me away.

I almost forgot about the bus and ran after it when it was moving away. The driver slowed down, 'All right, girl. The man who made time made plenty of it.'

An artificial-looking redhead with gluey eyelashes and high heels staggered on to the bus behind me. She wore a maroon-coloured coat trimmed with maroon-coloured fur and she smelt of port wine. A young skinhead was standing at the bus stop and he shouted after her, 'Go 'way, you flah bag.' His eyes were popping out of his head.

The bus conductor was giving out to the driver about something. 'Cat melodeon, the worst ever. In all my born days I never saw the bate of it. I mean to say like, it was cat. Cat! Cat! Cat!'

'Sounds bad, boy,' said the bus driver.

'You've no idea. Of course when the wife found out, like.'

I got out at the hospital and I still hadn't found out what was so cat. I walked around for a while. I was afraid to go in. Afraid to see Colette. Afraid that the matron would grab me. 'You're still not fat enough, you must stay here again.' Keep me there for all eternity, pumping me with fats and carbohydrates.

Colette was in a room with three middle-aged women. They looked very boring and they stared at me.

'Ah, it's Volunteer Jones!' Colette shouted. 'They all think I'm mad.' She pointed to the three women. They looked away quickly. 'Draw the curtains, dearie,' Colette mocked. 'Nosy old bats,' she said, when I had the curtains drawn and we were safely hidden in the blue rectangle. She was unrepentant. She lay back, 'You gave in to the bastards, but they'll never get me.' She tossed back her fair hair, it had grown darker but was still shiny, falling everywhere, slippy as soap.

'You'll never guess who was in to see me!'

'Who?'

'Your old music teacher.'

'Sister Marie Therese!' I had forgotten all about her.

'Came waddling in here last night, waving a big stick and ordering everyone about. She's in for tests.'

'What for?'

'Her digestion. According to herself there's nothing wrong with it. You should have heard her! Farting and belching and burping, it was an unbelievable performance. I'd say the convent made her come in. They must be really sick of it.'

'So was there any result?'

'I don't think they've found anything. She had a barium enema yesterday.'

'What's that?'

'They put a tube up your backside and pump you up with some kind of bicycle pump thing.'

'Really?'

'Oh I'd say it's just fantasy. She's living in another world. Do you know she had the cheek to tell *me* that I should have one of those barium enemas.'

'No!'

'I'm telling you. Said that it was *my* digestion that they should be investigating. Started pinching my arms, saying that I needed fattening.'

'What did you say?'

'I can't remember,' Colette said, crossly and folded her arms. 'Well, what did you bring me?' I gave her the book. 'Steinbeck! He went out with The Flood. What do I want to be reading that old eedjit for? I read only sex manuals now. I can have as much sex as I like. My periods have stopped completely. Of course the crowd here are fierce worried about them. They're afraid that I might never be able to have children! I told them that I'm very concerned. The old fools believed me.'

I laughed at her, she looked funny wagging her head on her stick neck and waving her wand arms. She was normal again. I gave her the cigarettes and chewing gum and Colette put on her sunglasses and beret before we went out to the bathroom together.

'The women are supposed to be keeping an eye on me, but they're too afraid of me to say anything.'

The women were huddled on one bed, their permed heads in a tight bunch. 'Lead the way, Volunteer,' Colette said. The women kept looking and then pretending that they weren't. 'Have you got the rifle?'

In the bathroom, Colette flung open the window and hung out, smoking in an exaggerated way.

'How're you managing with the food? I had to eat absolutely loads. I've got so fat.'

'Why didn't you make yourself sick?'

'They were watching me all the time. I couldn't.'

'Where there's a will there's a way,' Colette narrowed her eyes and stared at me very hard. Then, dancing around the bathroom, she started to laugh again very softly, 'Ha, ha, let's go into the mystic, ha, ha. You're not able for the pace, Volunteer Jones.' Her mouth was hard under the sunglasses.

I remembered the night Colette brought me up to the toilet in the top corridor. To show me how to make myself sick. I tried really hard, pushing down on the back of my tongue, like Colette had shown me. She said that I had to know how to to it. It was vital. I kept trying, saliva dripping down my fingers, while Colette held me tight around the waist, pressing hard on my stomach.

'There's a kind of a thing hanging down at the back of your throat, hit it a few belts or press it,' Colette said.

'I can't, I can't,' I was gasping, panicking as I

scrabbled at the back of my throat. Scraping it with my nails.

I felt such a failure when I couldn't do it. Colette could do it at the drop of a hat. Any time. After breakfast, just for the heck, even though she hadn't overeaten. It was surprising how much came up after eating just a half slice of bread.

'Do you know what that thing that hangs down at the back of your throat is called?' Colette had asked.

'I've no idea,' I had said impatiently.

'It's called your uvula.'

Colette started humming and singing *Into the Mystic* again. I had to get out. The cigarette smoke was irritating me and I was afraid that I was going to cry. There was a big gorge widening itself in my chest. I tried to kiss Colette. Half-heartedly. Colette gave me a penetrating look. 'You have failed, Volunteer Jones.'

I ran out of the bathroom, banging and clattering on the wide shiny staircase. Tripping on the last step, I crashed down, landing on my chin. Falling in public was the worst thing. Everybody was looking. I ran out. I imagined that I could still hear Colette singing *Into the Mystic.*

Desperate, haunting words about being younger than the sun and the wind and sailing off mysteriously.

I walked back to the centre of the city with my arms folded to keep everything in my chest. I mustn't let it out. All that crying. I was afraid that my mother would get me certified. I passed the Courthouse. Down Grand Parade and on to the South Mall.

She was waiting in the Imperial Hotel. In the orangery. A table was sunk into a kind of a green carpeted hole. She sat behind a pot of coffee. 'I don't think you'll need cakes for a while. It's very artificial isn't it? That weight you put on in the hospital. I'm sure you'll go back to normal soon.' She was trying to be nice.

'And how the fuck do you know?' I couldn't help bursting out, my chest all twisted and sore from crying. My heart was broken from the sight of myself in the glass.

Of course it was all right for her to cry. She wasn't worried about being put into an asylum. She was mortified at my bad language. Where had I learnt it? How could I come out with it in public? That Colette!

When she mentioned Colette, I started crying again and ran into the toilets. My mother came after me and put her arms around me.

'Feel your poor hands, they're frozen,' she said, and turned on the electric hand dryer to warm them up. She turned them round and round in the heat, but then someone came in and she dropped my hands quickly.

Back in the orangery, the coffee spilled in our saucers. We rested the cups on folded napkins to stop the drips.

'We'll do nice things for the summer holidays,' my mother said and twiddled the rings on her fingers. She had stopped looking at me.

· *Twenty-eight* ·

My mother and I were at the kitchen window, watching the rain. Drinking cups of Bovril. My mother found out that Bovril was low in calories. The cupboard was full of it. I was sick of it. All summer. Beefy and hot. Fucking Bovril.

I longed for a packet of crisps. Colette and I used to have them when we were having a breakout. Our salty fingers. Licking each grain from the crevices in our skin. I thought that it was better than sex. But I didn't tell Colette.

Sometimes I had cuts on my fingers and it was really brilliant when the salt stung deep.

'That's so good for you,' Colette used to say.

And I plunged my hand deep into the crackling bag. Showing off. Smiling instead of flinching.

'I'm so jealous!' Colette didn't get cuts on her fingers like I did. My skin was sensitive to the cold, it cracked and opened in the winter. Colette leaned against me hoping that the pain could be conducted through her like electricity.

Colette said that cracked skin was the sign of an early death and I hoped that she was right.

What an achievement.

'Drink up!' my mother said and I jumped guiltily. I didn't want her to guess that I was counting the weeks to September when I made up with Colette and we could start suffering again.

'We've got to go now, anyway. Catherine and Delia will be expecting us. Delia is so excited, she said she couldn't wait to see my face.'

'A glorious day,' my mother cried as she drove swiftly away. 'It's the height of the tourist season in Riverside,' her voice rose with the speedometer. 'You're going to have a great time with Delia.'

Burke had told my mother that I needed to be taken out of myself, mix more with people my own age during the holidays. 'In other words have the normal teenage experiences.' This was a bit difficult for my mother as she never allowed me out and I had no friends of my own age.

'Isn't Delia so good to be taking you out with her?' my mother said again.

I wished she didn't keep saying it. I felt bad enough being a burden, without being reminded about it.

But Delia didn't mind at all. 'I'm only looking forward to it,' she said, swinging her new page boy hairstyle.

She was wearing mascara. It really suited her. She sat on the edge of the sofa, her hands resting on her thin legs. Looking svelte and comfortable in her Levis. Mine were too tight and I kept putting my finger inside the button to ease the pressure. My mother gave my stomach a funny look.

'I'm only dying to get away for a good chat with Grace.' Delia never stopped surprising me with the things that she said.

I wanted to believe it was true. 'Thanks very much,'

I said and felt stupid. Fat. Conscious of my mother's fond face in the background.

Not admiring me.

Auntie Catherine went out to get the brown bread that Delia had baked specially for me. Noises came from the kitchen as Auntie Catherine banged cutlery and trays. She was awkward, but she got things done. My mother was graceful, but left a mess behind her. And nothing done.

'Your mother says that you have to watch your weight,' Auntie Catherine said. Her face red from the oven. 'But mind your health for God's sake, won't you?'

'She's fine now,' my mother said firmly. 'She's healthier looking than myself.'

'Well, I'm not going to eat any sweets or cakes while you're around,' Delia said.

'Now!' my mother said, looking fierce at me. And sweet at Delia. Auntie Catherine put her hand on Delia's arm.

'Mummy, don't forget the brown bread. It must be in fifty minutes at least.' Delia rushed her mother out of the kitchen.

'You've no idea how lucky you are! Nobody's got a cousin like Delia. She's the best girl I know.' My mother sat down on the armchair. 'I hope Catherine hasn't burnt the brown bread again.'

After dinner Delia came and sat beside me on the couch. 'Don't take any notice of them.'

I don't know why she said it because nobody had spoken to me during the whole meal. Except when my mother gave me a third helping of lettuce.

'I'll take you round Riverside. Do you want to go to see John Travolta?'

'Is *Grease* on?' I would be able to say I was at the pictures when I went back to Mayo.

'You are one lucky girl, that's all I can say,' my mother said. 'I didn't get to see a film until I was married and expecting you. We went to see *West Side Story.* I'll never forget it. I was as sick as a dog.'

We set off at seven o'clock, wheeling our bicycles. Following the path of the river that led to Riverside Bridge. It was too dangerous to cycle, the road was far too busy. Delia said. The river was broad and quiet, its banks were green. You couldn't help admiring it. And feeling peaceful.

We were almost there, when Delia threw her fashionable leg over the wall.

'What's happening?' I asked.

Delia landed with a thud on the other side of the ditch. 'Come on quick, hand over the bicycles before a car comes.'

The bicycles were heavy, but I didn't like to complain. When I raised each bicycle up, staggering under the weight, Delia grasped the saddle and handlebars. Then she caught my hand and pulled me over the wall. My feet jarred on the ground and I looked at the town which was getting smaller as she dragged me along the bank of the river.

'Is this a short cut to the Star Cinema?' I asked.

'It is in its arse! We're going to a party.'

'What will they say?'

'They won't know. They're going off to play cards. They won't be home until all hours.'

I followed dejectedly, my heart broken with disappointment. I wanted to go to *Grease.* I didn't want to go to a party, looking the way I did. In the cinema you could hide in the dark and eat crisps. And you forgot who you were while you were watching the film.

We came to a field dotted with tents. Music was playing loudly from a huge ghetto blaster.

'There, you can tell them you heard John Travolta,' Delia laughed as *Summer Days* came across the field.

'Jaysus, Delia, who's your one?' a tall fellow with long red hair and a Dublin accent asked her.

'My cousin, you'll have to be nice to her, Sam.'

'How about some pernod with red lemonade?' Sam asked, pulling out a whiskey bottle full of milky fluid.

'I don't drink,' I lied. They were all so old.

'Don't be such a fool, you'll only be laughed at,' Delia whispered into my ear.

I still wanted Delia to like me.

I looked around. A girl in a leather jacket was lying on the ground on top of a dark-haired man. They were kissing and groaning. I looked away embarrassed.

'All right so,' I said and took a drink. At least it tasted nice. But not as nice as crisps and popcorn and ice cream in a dark cinema.

Delia smiled at me. As if I was one of the gang or something.

'Ah, she's just sweet,' Sam drawled. He had horrible hard tobacco breath.

Delia lit a cigarette, puffing the smoke up past her fringe. Looking wicked and dangerous. I took a cigarette too. At least I would be able to tell Trish and Colette that I was at a party.

We went into a tent and a load of people were there wrenching at six packs of lager. Singing. It was so embarrassing, but Delia didn't mind. She wasn't scared or anything. Drinking, smoking, singing *Hey You Get Off Of My Cloud.* She knew all the words.

Sam kept pushing himself against me and it was horrible. His breath stank and his nose was awful, hooked, and a disgusting yellow colour as if it had been carved out of the leg of a chicken.

A fellow with a squashed looking face came in.

'Delia!'

'Eamon!'

She jumped up and ran to the opening of the tent. He caught her hand and the two of them kind of skipped away. I was on my own with Sam.

'He's an ugly fucker, isn't he?' Sam said, about Delia's friend. 'Jaysus, he's got a face like an elephant's arse. I don't know what she sees in him.'

I didn't either, it was a terrible shock to me. I had imagined Delia's boyfriends as having strong jaws and tweed jackets. Which was stupid when I thought about it. Fellows Delia's age didn't wear tweeds. They wore denim jackets and parallels.

After an hour of Sam and Sam's breath, feeling sick from pernod and lemonade and cigarette smoke, I staggered out of the tent. The night had got cold. I shivered and bumped into sleeping bags that were scattered around the field. Girls and men writhed and moaned. I thought I was going to die with the cold.

I found Delia under a tree kissing Elephant's-Arse-Face, pushing herself against him, inserting her leg between his knees. I was mortified. Rushed off into the dark field. It was a free country, she could do what she liked. But Jesus Christ! I couldn't take it. Not Delia with him! In that way.

I ran round in circles until I decided what to do. Then I went to the river, tripping over branches and brambles as I went. I found my bicycle. Somehow, I dragged it on to the road and set off in the direction of Auntie Catherine's house.

In the morning, a couple of Dutch tourists found me on the ground outside Riverside graveyard, crying over my wrist which had gone into an unnatural-looking curve.

Delia had been up all night, driven out of her mind with worry.

'Why did you run off on her like that?' My mother sat, crossing and uncrossing her leg, in the casualty department of Saint Michael's hospital. 'After all she did for you! Have you no gratitude?'

I held on to my brown bag of X-rays and said nothing.

'At least you're alive anyway,' my mother said.

'I'm glad you care,' I said sarcastically.

'Care!' said my mother, not realising that I was being sarcastic. 'You just couldn't believe the night I put down last night.' She tried to wring my good hand but she couldn't reach it.

'I'm safe now,' I said, trying to comfort her.

'Thanks to Delia!' she said.

I boiled for five minutes after that.

They put me into a very white room and a huge man with a red moustache came in. Roaring. He said that he was an orthopaedic surgeon and he wore a plastic apron. The nurses thought he was hilarious. He said that I would be all right before I was married and I was amazed that he couldn't think of something more unusual to say. I smiled anyway.

The plaster they put on my wrist was messy. They soaked white rolls in a bucket of water and white mud went everywhere as they rolled the soggy strips around my wrist. The nurse said it would come off in six weeks.

'Have you got that?' she bellowed. 'Six weeks. You're a very lucky young girl to escape so lightly. Driving around on your bicycle in the middle of the night, with drink taken. You could be dead!'

Six weeks. That meant that the plaster would be off by the end of August. I wouldn't even get to show it at Mayo. And I had thought Colette would be able to write funny things on it. Six weeks. I gazed down at my stricken thighs as they chafed in my too-tight Levis. I wished it was time to go back to Mayo. So I could meet Colette and Trish and read novels in the dark under my bedclothes. Dodge Mass. And get thin again.

· *Twenty-nine* ·

I went to Saint Joseph's the first night at Mayo. Colette's bed was made up. Trish's father had already brought Colette's stuff in his Merc. I hadn't seen him. I would have liked to have seen a millionaire gangster. I asked Trish what he was like. She said that he was short and fat. She never said much about the MacSweeneys. As if they embarrassed her or something.

Colette would come next week, after her hospital check up. Her blanket with all the colours was folded at the foot of her bed. Her cubicle was square and empty without her. The space was sharp. The poster of Che Guevara was hanging down at one corner. Last year, she used to spread her arms wide around the poster and kiss his shadowed face. Her fair head under his beret had reminded me of the straw man in *The Wizard of Oz*.

Trish shuffled up the corridor with a tin box. I knew what was in the box. The biscuits that Trish always baked with her mother. They were filled with three different colours of icing, raspberry pink, lime green and white.

'There's a man coming to show slides of Padre Pio in the hall.'

It seemed fierce sad. There were no plays in the hall any more. Just Colm ranting and raving about Padre Pio and his stigmata. No more acting. No more artistes. Paul was convinced that it was the acting had made us all thin.

She was really abusive in the refectory. Insulting girls. Telling them that they were too thin. Holding up fatties as examples of perfection. It was really embarrassing for those girls. You could see that they only wanted to hide themselves.

She was always at my table. 'I want to see you eating now, Grace Jones.'

I stuck my fork in a sausage.

'I said I want to see you eating, *now.* I have never met the likes of you for sheer stubbornness. You've driven half the girls in this school off their heads with your foolish example, yourself and Colette MacSweeney.'

I stuck forkfuls of chips into my mouth. My stomach heaved.

'I don't know if Colette MacSweeney will ever be strong enough to come back!'

What a thing to say! Staring with her Balor the Fomorian eye. Trying to wear me down with threats.

'And if she does, I hope you'll be helping her. Not putting her life in danger again.'

'Bitch,' I said when the refectory door was safely shut behind her.

But the first week came to an end and Colette didn't come back. Trish rang home but they knew nothing. I tried hard to get interested in study. But the only thing that really gripped me was covering novels in brown paper so that I could read them in class. I spent ages, cutting the paper straight as a die. Moulding it tight to my books. Writing my name with different coloured pencils. Writing *French Verbs* on the cover of *The Godfather.* And *Macbeth* on *The Audacious Adventuress.*

I knew that I was getting even fatter. Something had to be done before Colette came back. I felt panic like a hammer every night when I left the refectory. *You're a sad case,* I told myself one morning, looking in the glass. I could manage to avoid eating at other meals. It was supper that I couldn't manage to avoid. Not with Paul standing over me.

That night, I ate two platefuls of chips, just stuffing down the fat rectangles without tasting them.

'Glad to see you're coming to your senses,' said Paul.

'Good girl,' said Carmel.

I drank four glasses of water. 'That's right,' said Paul. 'Wash it all down.'

'Go easy,' said Carmel when I asked for a second pot of coffee.

Colette always said you needed to drink lots of liquids. That you had to talk to yourself over and over. That you had to punch your stomach. That you had to think of something really disgusting. That you never gave up.

If you wanted to make yourself sick.

My stomach was sloshing with liquid when I left the refectory. I was afraid I wouldn't be able. I was excited. And I had to get rid of Trish.

'You go on ahead, I'm going up to the dormitory to get a book.'

'I'll come, too.'

'It's okay, I'll only be about five minutes.'

'I'm only dying for a walk.'

'Why don't you go up the walks too?'

'God, there's no need to be so snappy.'

'I'm not snappy. Look, I just want to be on my own.'

'Well, go and be on your own!'

It was hard having to get rid of people. That's what it was like. But you never gave up. That's what Colette said.

I pushed past the new second-years, and said, 'Hi!' in a really bright voice. I rushed past Brenda before she could stop me.

I ran up the stairs quickly and into the blue bathroom on the middle corridor. It was in darkness, but the toilet door was locked. Someone was in there and they hadn't put the light on. I'd have to go to the top corridor. As I was leaving, I heard the retches. And water running in the hand basin. Gasps and sighs.

Someone else making herself sick.

I had to keep going. I ran up the last flight of the stairs, my legs breaking under me. I couldn't allow myself to think of anything else.

Leaning over the toilet, my face almost touched the cool porcelain. I forced my finger back against the thing at the back of my throat. It didn't take long now that I was serious about it. After a few minutes it came up. Again and again. My body tingled. I felt a rush of blood in my legs as my stomach emptied each time. My eyes streamed, I felt strong. I cleaned everything carefully and opened the small frosted window.

In the mirror my face was covered in blotches and my eyes were bloodshot. I smoothed my hand over my flattened stomach.

In Lourdes dormitory, I cleaned my face carefully with Johnson's baby lotion and, after washing my hands slowly and dreamily, rubbed my wrists with Patchouli oil. My throat was stinging where I had grazed it with my nails. But I was singing my own mystical song when I came out.

We've been haunted by the moon
We've been hunted by the sun
We've been around since the velvet dark
Long ago when coal was leaves

My skin was white again. Except for the red marks where my teeth had bitten into my knuckles. But no one would know. I hadn't felt so good since the time I got A in biology.

Stars have burned your sister soul
Right the way back to the unicorn
Silver mane over the golden shore
Sunbeams storing carbon in the trees

I was very proud of getting in the scientific bit about coal coming from fossilised trees. I couldn't help thinking that Van Morrison wasn't *that* knowledgeable.

I looked at my watch. I wasn't even late for study. Everything was fitting in. I would go down to study and open my neat brown-papered novel and read until bedtime.

I went downstairs slowly. Feeling thin and graceful. I stopped at the blue bathroom out of curiosity but it was empty. The windows were wide open and clean air was rushing in from the outside. You couldn't smell anything.

In study, I felt sleepy and I couldn't concentrate. My throat felt lumpy and I felt a bit down. At nine o'clock I collapsed into my bed.

I dreamt I was on the brass staircase and it was moving like an escalator towards the top corridor. I stood still as it carried me along. I passed Colette on the way, she was standing in a ravine and her face was turned away from me. As the stairs moved towards the top, they began to separate from the corridor and I was carried off sideways. It was horrible.

I awoke, perspiring. The cubicle stank of Patchouli oil. It was nauseating. I couldn't sleep. I was so hungry and my stomach growled and growled in the dark. There was an awful taste in my mouth. I got up and washed my teeth. I drank two glasses of water. Still my stomach growled. I was awake for ages, listening to taps dripping and trying to pretend that I didn't have a fierce pain in my stomach.

· *Thirty* ·

In the morning I felt unbearably tired. I could hardly keep my swollen eyes open. The whole skin of my body felt puffy and awful, as if I needed to shed it. Carmel called me early. I had my eyes tightly shut as I climbed out of bed, waiting for her to go on to call the other girls. When I opened them, Sister Carmel was still there, her face earnest.

She put her arms around me. 'Colette died in her sleep last night.'

I was disgusted. 'I'm surprised at you, Sister Carmel, to tell such desperate lies!'

Sister Carmel held me tightly and I lay against her chest. I could smell the baby talc that she wore and her cross was hard against my cheek. I didn't want to be held so tightly. I felt suffocated but I suffered it for Carmel's sake.

Carmel took out a flask and two of the little white pills they had fed me before. I took them numbly. I hardly felt the light pills on my tongue. But the taste of the water was hard and metallic. I gulped it down. My throat hurt.

'You must try to bear this big cross,' Sister Carmel said. 'And I know you're very young, love.'

She had never called me *love* before. It sounded weird.

'The removal is tonight and the funeral is tomorrow, it will be very hard on her family.' I put my head on her chest again. I felt her chest rise and fall, and matched my breathing to the rhythm.

Later, in the afternoon, Carmel came and spent an hour with me. I was afraid that she would start going on with some baloney about Colette being gone to Heaven, but she did not talk about Colette at all. She spoke about herself. She had grown up on a small farm in County Sligo. They had six acres and six cows. She got up at six every morning to feed them. *Six six six.* The number of the Beast. I knew that's what Colette would be thinking if she was there. I had a terrible time trying not to laugh.

Most of her family had emigrated to England to look for work. They all wrote to her except Michael, her youngest brother. And he was her favourite. She was afraid that he might be too lonely to write.

I wondered if she had ever been lonely. I asked her when she had joined the convent. Sister Carmel had joined the order in 1947 when she was sixteen. She said that she had been happy with God ever since.

I believed that she meant it and thought about it for a long time that night as I tossed around my bed. Could you think you were happy and not be happy? Lots of people said that you never realised you were happy until afterwards. And how could you be happy if you didn't know it. People usually said that your school days were the best days of your life. If I was having the best days of my life, I didn't know it.

I decided if you were happy then you had to realise

it, so if Sister Carmel said she was happy then there was a good chance that she was. But then again she may have been just trying to make me feel better.

I thought about how Colette pretended to be funny but she hadn't been really. Then I was afraid her ghost might appear to me. '*We knew you'd give us a good laugh,*' I remembered Colette saying, the time they left the statues outside Saint Joseph's.

I threw the blankets over my head and sweated. I wondered why the pills weren't working. I just wanted to sleep. I tossed and turned listening to the creaks of the other beds, to the snores and moans of all the other girls in Nazareth. I was kind of annoyed with them all for sleeping when Colette had just died. And kind of pleased that I was the only one awake.

I wondered should I start praying and all the rest of it. I heard that some of the girls were doing a novena to Our Lady. No wonder they were sleeping soundly. Feeling safe.

I would have liked to feel safe too.

We had to go to Colette's funeral to form a guard of honour. We passed MacSweeney's house. It was very big. White. And it was called *Gracelands.* No wonder Colette never gave me her address. I was half looking forward to seeing her parents. And I was really looking forward to seeing Johnny. I kept having these stupid daydreams, Johnny saying that he was in love with me, Mr MacSweeney writing me out a cheque for a thousand pounds, or Mrs MacSweeney giving me the keys of her BMW and teaching me to drive.

When I saw Mrs MacSweeney, I knew she wasn't the BMW type. Her tan looked weird and wrong, especially with her face all saggy with grief. She was like my Auntie Catherine. Rich by mistake.

And Mr MacSweeney didn't know any of us. He only

knew Trish and he could hardly speak to her. When I saw him struggling and swallowing and trying to keep his head up in the funeral parlour, I found I had a lump in my throat too.

Seeing Colette was awful. I started really crying. And I didn't have to suppress my imagination about BMWs and cheques for a thousand pounds. I thought about her body rotting and how it would end up as nothing. I couldn't bear it. Some eedjit had put blue eyeshadow on her eyelids. Her face was yellow and it was set like plaster. I wanted to die too and I couldn't stop crying.

When I was at the coffin, I heard the whispers, 'Johnny, Johnny, where is Johnny?' They echoed in my head. I wondered had he committed suicide. I couldn't kiss Colette's forehead because I had felt it with my finger and it was too cold. I knew it wasn't Colette. I touched her blonde hair where it touched the blue silk lining. It was the same as before. Soft like a baby's. But hair was dead anyway.

When Johnny arrived, the crowd should have parted but it didn't. It broke up into a confused mess. That was because everyone was looking at him. His head was shaved. It looked a kind of dark grey colour. His eyes were red. He was wearing huge boots. I looked at Mr and Mrs MacSweeney, but they acted like it was normal. I couldn't figure out whether they didn't mind. Or whether they didn't want to let on that they minded. I backed away with the rest of the crowd.

He smiled at me.

Mr MacSweeney and Johnny carried the coffin with two of Colette's cousins. The cousins had short haircuts and big ears. They looked like Mormons. I thought that Colette must have teased them like mad. I wondered were they pleased that Colette was dead.

I wanted to throw myself into the coffin too. Mr MacSweeney started crying when they were lowering the coffin. Awful sounds. I can still hear them. The nearest thing I can think of is a seal barking.

The Guard of Honour was invited back to *Gracelands.* A big long dining table was piled up with everything. Sandwiches, quiches, vol au vents, salads. Paul came with us and stood with a huge plate, talking to Mr MacSweeney. She was a head taller than him. He looked worn out.

'If only she'd been made to do more sport!' I heard him saying to Paul.

Paul looked savage, but she couldn't attack the chief mourner. She swept a few more vol au vents into her mouth and chewed angrily. Her eyebrows completely joined up over her Balor the Fomorian eye.

'Lack of sport, that's all that was wrong with her,' Mr MacSweeney kept on.

I went to find the bathroom. There were loads. They were all too big. I kept searching because I was looking for a small one. I didn't feel safe in the big ones. Or maybe I was just looking for Johnny. I met him at the top of the stairs. And then I forgot what I was supposed to be looking for.

There was a mad look in his eye. Mad with grief, I thought.

'She would have died anyway. She had a weak heart. It could have gone at any time. Had it since birth.'

I had heard that she only had a bad heart because she had starved herself. Everyone said it. Not just Paul, but Trish and Carmel. Loads of people. I looked at him. He started chewing the skin at the side of his finger.

'I see you're looking as beautiful as ever.'

I thought that I was going to go right off him. There was a portrait of Mrs MacSweeney behind him. It was nice and she didn't have that awful tan. It must have been done before she bought the sunbed or maybe the painter had toned it down. She had her gardening gloves on. A trowel in her hand.

'I'm really sorry about Colette.'

'I know you are. You were her best friend.'

I liked him again. A strange film of moisture was gathering over his face. He wiped it off with his handkerchief. And gave me a penetrating look. Then closed his eyes for a minute. I began to get uneasy. What if someone saw me speaking to him? Paul. Or one of the girls. I looked around.

'Do you want to see Colette's bedroom?' His eyes were open again and he was staring.

'If it's okay?' At least I would be out of view.

There was such a strong smell of Indian perfume in Colette's bedroom. Patchouli, Jasmine, Sandalwood and Franjipani. It was fierce sad. I saw Colette's carved Indian box where she kept all the little bottles. We used to pick a different one for every night we spent together. We used to have Patchouli nights, Jasmine nights, Sandalwood nights. Franjipani nights were a bit sickening. Too sweet. There were Indian scarves everywhere.

'You've got to excuse me.' He talked as if I was in control. As if he had to impress me. 'I'm just totally wasted.'

'God, I'm sure you are tired.'

'No, wasted.'

'Wasted.'

'Do you know what wasted means?'

'I think I've heard of it. Although, I suppose I don't know. What is it?'

'Wasted from drugs. Been popping things like mad.'

'Cannabis,' I said knowledgeably.

'I don't count cannabis as a drug.' He lay down on the bed. 'I've been on acid, man.'

I thought then that I was fed up with being impressed. He looked at me with his eyes half open. Slanty. And smiled. He looked just like Colette.

'Come here.'

I went over to the bed and he caught my hand. 'I know all about you and Colette.' His hands were on my shoulders. I was dying for him to kiss me. He didn't. Just put his fingers on my lips. I could smell the tobacco. Then he pulled me on top of him. I kept thinking, I must get up. Someone's going to come in. They'll be looking for me. But it felt brilliant. He held me really tight. His arms were like iron.

He let me go. I got up awkwardly feeling a bit cold. He sat up and lit a cigarette. I noticed *Our Bodies Ourselves* on the locker.

'That was a great help, kid.'

I sat on the edge of the bed. Looking at him.

'Well, you better get back to the fold, I suppose,' he said, looking exhausted.

I felt awful. I ran to the door.

'And hey!'

'Yes?'

'That kiss was from Colette.' He smiled and sank back on the pillows, watching me. I smiled back even though it was killing me. As if I knew all the time. But the tears were close behind my eyes. I waved and closed the door behind me. On the corridor, I swallowed hard and saw my woebegone face in a huge oval mirror. I looked really hurt.

Jesus, that annoyed me! I went down the stairs, savage. His hair was horrible shaved anyway. At least I'd never see his face again. I was going straight to Paris when I finished school. I was only trying to be nice to him anyway. I should never have gone into that room.

'Wait!' he shouted suddenly from the top of the

stairs. I hadn't heard him coming out of the room. He must have crept out and it frightened the hell out of me.

'What?' I said, looking around furtively. There was no sign of anybody.

Johnny swayed at the top of the stairs. 'I know about Sister Carmel too,' he slurred.

'Know what?' I half shouted.

Johnny threw back his head and winked slowly. A sinister smile crept across his face.

'What's that supposed to mean?' I tried to keep shouting back but my voice had begun to falter.

Johnny's eyes got slittier, he looked more and more like Colette.

I had to hold on to the banister to support myself.

'She must die,' he said and began to feel the left pocket of his jeans. 'I'm going to cut out her fat heart.'

I watched his hand stroking his Levis, but I couldn't see the print of a knife in his jeans. Surely he was joking.

'She hasn't got a fat heart!' I felt stupid saying that.

'Of course you would know.' Johnny put his hands in the pockets of his jeans. It was hard for him to do, because his jeans were so tight. I didn't know where he'd get the room for a knife as well.

But I couldn't bear to hear him say another word against Carmel. 'Look here, Buster.' I started pounding my palm with my fist.

Johnny looked at me and I saw how red his eyes were from crying. I felt sorry then. 'Oh fuck off, you,' I sobbed and ran back to the Guard of Honour party.

Going back on the bus, there were sobs and moans and snuffles, while the windows of the bus showed big black trees then yellow streetlamps, then big black trees again and the odd lighted house on the country roads between towns. Paul gave out the rosary. Everyone was crying.

I couldn't help feeling that I'd been too hard on Johnny. It was obvious that he was crazed with grief. But why bring Carmel into it? And why had Colette spoken about Carmel? Colette had never liked her, that worried me. Maybe Johnny blamed her for Colette's death. I was the only one who wasn't crying on the bus. I was too frightened.

· *Thirty-one* ·

Carmel said that we were to let it all out, but she kept passing on the white pills from Paul. I tried not to think about Colette and it helped. If I thought about Colette, I thought about Johnny. And I couldn't bear it.

And every time I saw Carmel, I hated Johnny. Carmel's delicate small puffy chest rustling inside the black nylon housecoat. Her little heart! How could he have even said such a thing. I looked up 'the heart' in my biology book. It was true that the heart was protected by a layer of fat. I imagined Carmel's heart covered with pure white fat. Like an altar candle. I was haunted by the image of Johnny cutting through her black clothes. Her surprised face. Johnny smiling. It was like a black mass. I was afraid to go to sleep at night and when I knelt over the toilet to get sick, I kept imagining the devil was going to catch me by the scruff of the neck.

Later that week, Trish and I were sent to Coolin woods on a botany trip. Carmel was putting in all these special pleas for us. And Paul was listening to her.

The Friday night before we went we collected all the blue colour pencils we could find. We got seven different shades, mostly from the first-years. Brenda Driscoll gave me some brown pencils. They were all different and they were kind of nice, but they weren't blue. I hated having to change things, especially when I said that all the bark rubbings in our botany project were going to be blue.

'And what's wrong with brown and blue?' Brenda asked.

I thought that she was being very cheeky. 'Give them to me,' I said, in an authoritative voice. 'I'll see what we can do with them.'

Trish and I went for a walk before breakfast, excited at the thought of getting the bus all by ourselves. We walked past the stream where I had tried to commit suicide. It reminded me of Colette, I felt weak and sat down on the grass.

'*It's All Over Now, Baby Blue*,' I began singing in a desperate weak cracked voice. I didn't want to in front of Trish but I couldn't stop.

'It's all right,' said Trish and put her arm around me. That made me cry. She had to take me back and I felt really stupid in front of the first-years who were hanging around the lower corridor, staring. They couldn't help looking, I was such an exhibition.

'Go on up to the dormitory, I'll bring up trays,' Carmel said, waving the onlookers into the refectory for breakfast.

I stopped crying when Carmel came with the tray and we had loads of toast and honey. I was gone off cornflakes. Then I had to send Trish down to the study for our botany folders while I made myself sick. I felt fine then and I was getting really good at it. I was singing *It's All Over Now, Baby Blue* when Trish came back. But singing it in a different way.

*

We wore our Levis and our check shirts, we had our folders and our colouring pencils, we were a half an hour early for the bus and sitting in the sun, when I remembered the brown pencils.

I had to run really hard and when I reached the study, Brenda Driscoll was waiting for me with her arms folded.

'Haven't you forgotten something?' She couldn't have sounded more important.

'Right, right, right! You've got my pencils. Hip, hip hooray!' I grabbed them off her. I was going to have to get very strict with her. She was acting like she owned me.

I walked off without even saying thanks. I thought that should fix her.

'Wait!' Brenda wasn't a bit taken aback.

'What is it now?'

She waved a yellowy-white envelope. 'There's a letter as well.'

'Where did you get that?'

'Colm just put the post in the tray, I was coming to give it to you.'

Black loopy writing whirled across the envelope. 'Thanks,' I said, forgetting to be short with her as I ran off.

'Be sure and tell me what's in it!' Brenda called after me. I pretended that I hadn't heard her.

The paper was thick and luxurious. Rich. I turned it over, there was a name and address written in the top right-hand corner. *Mr MacSweeney, Graceland, Ballysand, Co Cork.* Why was Colette's father writing to me? He was a fierce, important person. He'd had breakfast with the Shah of Persia. I ripped the envelope open.

Dear Grace,
I've written the ould fella's name and address on the back to prevent suspicion falling on you. I think we understand each other and I want to follow it up. I want to tell you how Colette really died and I know who was to blame too. We both do.
I'll be coming to see you soon,
Love, Johnny.

My first thought was that he was coming to get Carmel . . . *I want to follow it up . . . I know who was to blame . . .* My heart began to go mad and I shivered. By now I was standing at the top of the avenue and Trish was shouting and waving her arms. The bus was coming. I stuffed the letter into my pocket and ran down.

'What kept you?' Trish's face was hot and worried-looking.

'Oh, it was just Brenda, she had the pencils.'

'Why didn't she just hand them over and stop talking for once?' Trish started biting her nails the way she did when she was annoyed.

'You know what she's like,' I said, wondering should I tell Trish. It would ruin my chances of an affair with Johnny if I did. And he probably didn't mean it anyway.

I didn't say a word to Trish. We spent the morning doing bark rubbings. They looked beautiful when we had finished, pale blues, soft and deep blues burning, filling the pages, and then the browns in between, looking horsy and expensive.

We stopped for lunch and lay in the sun, eating the ham sandwiches Carmel had prepared for us. Trish unrolled a bundle of fig rolls.

'I'm sure she robs them from the convent stores,' Trish said.

'I know.' I was stabbed by a picture of Johnny and Carmel struggling behind the pantry door.

'She's probably afraid of getting caught.'

'But who would suspect her?' I was outraged at the idea. It was nearly as bad as Johnny saying that she had a fat heart.

'Well, I did and you just agreed with me.'

I couldn't eat the fig rolls because there was nowhere private for me to get sick. The ham sandwich was sitting heavy now. I thought of pigs and their flesh. And trotters and snouts. I wished I had eaten a cheese sandwich. Pigs squealing in agony as their throats were cut.

'Are you okay about Colette now?' Trish asked.

I sighed, thinking about Johnny.

'Johnny is supposed to be gone really bad,' Trish said.

'How do you mean?'

'Weirder and taking drugs. I wouldn't be surprised if he ends up in Saint Anne's again.'

'How do you mean again?'

'Well, you know he's mad don't you?'

'What do you mean by mad?'

'You know, loopy, loony, a penny short of a shilling!'

'Oh! But Colette never . . . why didn't you say?'

'I thought you knew. It's not that bad, he gets around and he's not a psychopath or anything.'

'He's not violent?' I tried to act nonchalant, but my voice was shaking.

'Johnny? He wouldn't hurt a fly. He used to run away from all the fights at National school. You're not thinking of going out with him, are you?'

'No, God, no! No way! Jesus, what do you think I am?'

'It's all right then. Actually he's a bit of a laugh if you don't rely on him or anything.'

Trish blew up her fringe and looked at me. 'He's on lithium, you know.'

'Lithium? That's in the Periodic Table of Elements!'

'I know.'

'It's an alkali metal.'

'I know, that will give you an idea of how mad he is, girl.'

Lithium was a soft metal. Sister Assumpta cut it with a knife. There were sticks of lithium in a jar of solution in the science lab. When she cut the stick, the metal showed up bright and shining. It discoloured real quick though. Oxidised when it was exposed to the air. I remembered it from my scientific days. I couldn't help thinking that it was exciting, now that I knew he wasn't violent. Johnny was on *lithium.*

The sun got very strong and we moved all our equipment under a wide spreading tree. I decided that I was never going anywhere without a bathroom again. I couldn't eat in peace, if I couldn't manage to get sick.

'What kind of a tree is that?'

'Lime.'

'I think it's beech.'

'Well, why did you ask so?'

The wind blew and the leaves whitened as they moved in the sunlight. We drew our plant cross-sections.

'A pity we didn't collect a load of greens as well.'

'Yes, do you think there's forty shades of green?'

'I'd say there's away more.' I decided that I liked Johnny better because he was mad. Anyone could be sane.

We examined each other on the phloem and xylem parts. We traced the path of the nutrients and oxygen through their tubular conducting systems and impressed each other with what we had learnt.

'We're completely dependent on plants for photosynthesis, it's kind of spooky when you think about it.'

Trish gave a kind of shivery nod, 'I saw a programme on television once where this woman had a really brilliant garden. She could grow anything in it and do you know why?'

'No, why?'

'There had been an abattoir on the land for a couple of hundred years and it was all that blood that made the flowers grow.'

'I suppose plants are cannibals really when you think about it.'

'They can't be cannibals.'

'Well, savages or something. You know what I mean. They're not as innocent as they look.'

We were quiet for a while. I went for a run to work off the ham sandwich. Later, Trish thought she saw a fox and we followed its fluttering rusty colour down a long track. As we ran I thought about Carmel and Johnny again. Maybe Trish was wrong, she wasn't infallible. Maybe he was going to become violent from the pressure of Colette's death. Then I thought about Johnny's thin iron arms around me and the glamorous smell of cigarettes and drugs. I decided it was okay in a shaky sort of way.

At the end of the day, we stood out on the road to catch the country bus back to Mayo. The sun was still shining. I ate fig rolls on the bus. We went back to the dormitory to put our drawings and rubbings away. I hung some of the heavenly blues and horsy browns over my bed. And arranged pine cones on the shelf over my sink. I drank loads of water and went to the bathroom to get rid of the fig rolls. I was singing again when I came out.

Stars have burned your sister soul
Right the way back to the unicorn

Silver mane over the golden shore
Sunbeams storing carbon in the trees

· *Thirty-two* ·

Sister Carmel and Trish didn't like me going into the mystic. They used to call me back by asking questions and forcing me to answer them. Trish put her head very close to mine and looked into my eyes, saying, 'Hello, is there anyone in there?'

It drove me mad.

Sister Carmel was worse in a way. She was very gentle and didn't shout the way Trish did. She just stood there and wouldn't go away until I answered her questions. Sighing, and rubbing her little hands on her crackly housecoat, until I had to respond.

Making me feel mad and guilty.

'What would you like for supper, I'll bring a tray to your room.'

'Why don't you write a little letter to your mother?'

'Why are you getting so thin, again?'

'You are eating, aren't you?'

And I kept wondering about Johnny. Should I show Trish the letter?

My throat hurt like mad. I scraped it every time I made myself sick. I was always in a hurry, Trish was always on my heels. But I wanted to hurt myself too.

And all the feelings that overwhelmed and confused me disappeared when I made myself sick.

I didn't mind about my throat getting cut. It seemed right. Like I deserved it. I wouldn't have minded getting scraped away altogether. I imagined myself as a white wraith meeting Johnny in the convent woods.

Mystical.

Trish annoyed me, making me talk to her all the time. I didn't show it, it was just another thing I had to send down the toilet with the undigested chips.

The food came out of my stomach looking very much as it did when it went in. I always had the food back up within a half an hour of eating it. It wasn't disgusting.

'Thanks be to God!' I said to the mirror and put my two hands inside the waistband of my skirt.

Sometimes I said 'Fuck Johnny.' I didn't like the way he was ruining everything. What took it into his head to abuse Carmel? Colette used to tease me about Carmel, maybe she told him that Carmel was my sex kitten.

Surely he was just teasing me. Before he took me in his arms and I went into the mystic. Johnny's crooked tooth, his knee between mine, his faded Wranglers, the crazed look in his eyes.

Mysterious.

There was one good thing and that was botany. Trish and I were into it. Drawing cross-sections, colouring them in and sticking them up on the walls of our cubicles.

'It's peaceful,' I said to Trish, shading a spyrogyra pale green.

'Green is a very restful colour.'

'Calming.'

'Yes and cooling.'

'Like aquariums.' I cunningly moved the subject on. 'It's a wonder they don't have them in mental asylums.'

'Aquariums?'

'Yes.'

'You're obsessed with the mental. It's unhealthy.'

'I'm not.'

And then I couldn't say anymore.

Trish talked about Colette sometimes. But she never talked about Johnny. I couldn't understand it. The living link.

Then one night, I had a desperate fight with Trish. In the blue bathroom. Brenda Driscoll was there as well, her red hair standing out with surprise. That's what really got to me. Her listening to every word. I had only eaten a small bit of scrambled egg for supper, but I'd got used to being completely empty. I liked going to bed with a growling stomach. It was pure even if it was a bit loud. I drank four pints of water and went upstairs after supper. Trish followed me, pretending to be chatty.

I knew what she was up to. She knew I wanted to make myself sick and she was trying to delay me. If my supper got to my small intestine I was finished. The longer I left it, the harder it became. I hated her. Telling some stupid story about Sister Marguerite being an heiress, about her getting a red sports car for her eighteenth birthday, and leaving dozens of suitors weeping at the gates of the convent when she joined up.

'I don't give one fucking fuck about Sister Marguerite!'

'Grace!'

Brenda gave a small snigger, she peered out from behind the door of the airing cupboard.

'Your language is gone very bad.' Trish's face went a horrible dark red.

'Fuck my language. What's wrong with it?' I imagined Johnny's face. Listening to me. Impressed.

'It makes you sound thick and you're not.'

'Well, thanks very much. I need you to tell me.'

'You're supposed to be really good at English,' said Brenda, trying to be nice.

'Shut the fuck up you!' said Trish, like a complete savage.

'Listen to yourself!' I said, thinking about all the eggs, disappearing down the plughole of my stomach.

'Well, I can't bloody help it. I'm not a saint.'

Brenda held her blue towel against her chest. And folded her arms over it. Getting comfortable.

'Go for your bath!' I said.

'Leave her alone,' said Trish.

'God, you should listen to yourself. At least I haven't used bad language to her.'

'Look, why won't you go back to study?' Trish tried to talk in a reasonable voice.

'Why should I? Why don't you?'

'Because I'm watching you.'

'Well, I'm glad you've admitted it. At long last!'

'It's not my blooming idea! I'm sick of it all. Vomit, vomit, vomit. You'd think you'd have learned from Colette.'

'Whose idea was it? Paul's? God, I never thought that you'd be like that.'

'It wasn't Paul's idea. You know I'd never talk to her.'

'So whose idea was it?'

'I'm not telling. It just happens to be someone who likes you. God only knows why!'

'I know who it was! Carmel!'

But Trish wouldn't say. She stood under that awful wide white lampshade with the blood darkening her face. Her black sheets of hair like funeral blinds. Biting her lips.

'Ah, Jesus, girls, you'll have to sort it out,' said Brenda Driscoll.

The bloody size of her. The cheek of it. I couldn't believe she was butting in. Before I'd speak to leaving certs like that . . .

But I didn't say one word. I had my fist clenched on my abdomen. Just where I thought my stomach joined the small intestine.

The duodenal cap lies to the right of the spine and the duodenal loop extends across the upper abdomen to the duodenal-jeunal flexure which lies in the left hypochondrium, behind the stomach.

I pressed harder where I thought the duodenal cap was.

Trish pulled my hand away from my stomach.

'Stop it,' I said and clamped it back quickly. As if my stomach had sprung a leak.

'I think she's got pain.' Brenda had moved close, tilting her face into mine, as if I was a baby in a pram.

'She's trying to make herself sick!' said Trish.

'I'm not, I'm trying to keep it in!' I was berserk.

Brenda was moving closer and closer.

'I can't see with your fucking hair!' I shouted.

'Look, I think you'd better take that bloody bath,' Trish said to her.

And Brenda went into one of the cubicles. Really slowly. And came out again immediately.

'Has anyone got the loan of some bubble bath?'

'No, do we look like it?'

And Brenda said, 'It's all right.' Her voice wasn't wounded or anything.

'I've got sandalwood bathsalts in my locker in Lourdes. You can take them if you like,' I said, still clasping my stomach.

'Why do you have to go pandering to her? You don't owe her bathsalts!'

'I'll give her what I like. At least she's gone. Which is more than you are.'

Trish banged out of the bathroom then. 'I've given up on you for good this time!'

'*You* have given up on *me*?' I shouted after her.

There was only silence and I rushed into the toilet quickly. Not a bloody hope. The four pints of water had gone on from my stomach. There wasn't enough momentum left with what I had. I scrabbled at my sore throat and spat up some blood. I stared at the white walls and blue wainscot.

I had had my bath nights here with Colette.

I bent over the toilet again. My fingers pushed, but nothing came. My mouth seemed to resist my fingers. I couldn't keep them inside any longer. My throat ached. I sat on the floor. Hating Trish. Looking at the wide white lampshade. It would have made a good hat for Sister Paul. It would have suited her ponderous face and her personality.

I heard Brenda trip back into the bathroom. I thought that I'd better stand up, but I couldn't be bothered. Or was too tired or something. I kept thinking about Trish's dark red angry face.

'There you are,' said Brenda, coming in with the orange box of bathsalts.

'Here I am,' I said, trying to sound jokey and in control.

But my heart was broken with the thought of that scrambled egg coursing its way to my thighs. I really couldn't stand the thought of any food getting around my body. It annoyed me. The way a person would. The way Trish did.

'I'm glad Trish is gone,' Brenda said, putting the bathsalts down on the floor and kneeling beside me.

'So am I,' I said. But I felt rotten.

'Are you very weak?' asked Brenda in a kind of adoring voice.

'I'm okay,' I said.

Brenda leaned towards me and whispered, 'Will you show me how to make myself sick?'

I stared back at her. I tried to speak, but I couldn't. Her two green eyes were on me like torches. I burst into tears.

'I'm sorry, I'm sorry. I didn't mean it. I know you don't. I thought that you might remember it. They were saying that Colette showed you how to do it.'

I was really bawling then. After she'd said Colette's name.

'I'm sorry, I'm sorry, I shouldn't have mentioned Colette.'

Brenda put her arm around me and shifted her legs, kicking the box of sandalwood bathsalts on to its side. There was pale orange powder all over the place.

'Oh no!'

I put my hand on Brenda's arm. 'Don't say you're sorry. I don't like sandalwood anyway.' This wasn't true and then I said, 'Look, I don't make myself sick either. It's really stupid.'

It was the only thing I could say. I couldn't tell a second-year that I thought it was great and I did it all the time. Especially after I'd been in charge of Brenda's dormitory last year.

Brenda was quiet for a while.

'Look, you're skinny anyway. You don't need to learn.'

'Neither do you.'

'I just told you that I don't!'

'I know. You couldn't go anywhere with it. They were

saying Colette always had to be within fifty yards of the loos. Or she turned into an antichrist.'

'It's no life,' I said. 'Come on, fill your bath. And keep the rest of the box.'

We found a dustpan and brush in the cupboard. Carmel had them stowed everywhere. It was kind of nice cleaning up together. And the woody sweet smell steaming out of Brenda's bath.

But I was too afraid to go near Trish. I was afraid that she wouldn't speak to me any more. It was nearly as bad as the scrambled egg. My throat seared and kept me awake. I was crying for ages and ages. It was one of the worst nights. I even forgot to think about Johnny.

· *Thirty-three* ·

I woke up feeling desperate. I was relieved when I remembered that I'd only had one third of a bowl of scrambled egg for my supper. Then I remembered Trish and I felt desperate anyway. I waited for her to come looking for me.

She didn't. But Brenda Driscoll did. Arrived in my dormitory at quarter past seven with her beret like a frisbee sitting straight on top of her springy red hair. I didn't know what to say. I felt guilty because I must have encouraged her in some way. And yet at the same time, I didn't think that I had.

Coming to collect someone for Mass was a really big thing. You had to be close. Colette was the only one before. Except for the time we broke it off. Since Colette died, Trish came. But that was different, a kind of compassionate thing.

I hovered, waiting for Trish. But I didn't let on to Brenda. I pretended that I couldn't get my beret straight.

'Your hair is so silky,' she sighed, lying back on my folded rug.

Jesus, she was worrying me. I wouldn't be able to do anything. I had been hoping to start on early-morning laxatives after mid-term. Colette said they were really brilliant when your metabolism was slowing down.

Trish's compassion must have run out. The bell was going at half past seven and she still hadn't come. I didn't let on a bit to Brenda.

'After you,' I said, swishing back the door of my cubicle with a debonair flick of my hand.

'Trish will hardly come now,' Brenda said, as she slid my door shut.

Trish didn't look my way once during Mass. It was a special Mass for Padre Pio or someone. Rosario had laid on a load of hymns. I liked hymns but I never let on. Hymns made me sentimental. I got a lump in my throat and my heart turned into an accordian. It only happened if they were sung by girls or nuns. Only those kind of voices had that effect. It was like you were being assumed into Heaven, with a brand new pair of wings but had to leave all your friends behind. They were singing 'Star of The Sea'. That was my favourite.

'*Pray for the wanderer, pray for me.*'

Brenda had a very bad voice. I was surprised that she hadn't been told about it. Then I realised she was doing it on purpose and cracking up laughing half the time. A couple of the other second-years were doing it as well. I couldn't have laughed if you'd paid me. I worried that maybe I was getting old. In the end, I went up to communion. To avoid an embarrassing situation.

I thought I'd get into a different seat on my way back, but faltered when I realised I was turning into Trish's seat. She didn't bat an eyelid. I got in because I couldn't turn back. And I didn't look at her once after that. The worst thing was that I was sitting right in front of Paul and I was conscious of her pale fat pillar of a face behind me the whole time.

Trish didn't come near me at breakfast time.

The whole day dragged. Terrible. I hardly ate, so there was no need to make myself sick. But I did anyway. Had to keep up the practice. I could do it so easily now. It was a shame to waste my talent. And I was only just in time. Brenda came thundering into the bathroom as I was washing my hands.

'Trish is gone up to the dormitory, do you want to follow her?'

'No, not particularly.' My voice was really sarcastic.

'Ah, you must. You can't be like this after Colette dying. It's scaring the hell out of me.'

'Well, okay, okay, if you insist.' I dried my hands carefully. Turning them round and round in the hot air of the drier. I didn't realise it was so enjoyable. I turned them round again.

Brenda started sniffing. 'Jesus, there's a desperate smell, it reminds me of Colette. Are you sure you're not making yourself sick?'

I took my hands out of the drier. 'Of course I'm sure, it's really thick.

'Like bad language.'

'There's no need to get smart.'

'I'm not getting smart. You haven't said fuck once since Trish said it was thick.'

Brenda was really getting on my nerves. Who did she think she was? A bloody psychiatrist?'

'I'd better go.'

'Are you sure you're not making yourself sick?'

'Are you a spy?'

'I'm not honestly, I just want to know.'

'Why?'

'Because I want to look like you.'

I wanted to laugh. Brenda's legs were so thin, and she wanted to look like me.

'I'm not making myself sick! OKAY?'

'All right, all right. Actually, I'm glad you're not, because it's awful hard work.'

'What do you know about it?'

'Some of the other second-years are doing it. They were trying to show me.'

'Who?'

'I can't say, but they all go over to the back bathroom at about twenty past seven. It's really spooky and dark. I forgot they were there once, and I went up to the loo. All the doors were locked and the taps going. But you could hear them choking and coughing. The wind was whistling like anything.'

'The wind had nothing to do with it,' I said, but I couldn't stop shivering.

'It didn't half. I never heard anything so lonely. I wanted to throw my arms around someone. Someone like you.' Brenda half dived, half swooned at me.

I held her for a few seconds, it was fierce nice. But I let her go fairly quickly. I didn't want Colm coming around and getting the wrong idea.

'Go for your bath, I'll go and check Trish out,' I said in what I hoped was an ordinary voice.

But I didn't go to Trish's cubicle. I went up to the back bathroom and then I ran crying all the way to Trish's cubicle. As I ran, the tears seemed to run down my throat and the salt burned the cut that never healed. The cut that I opened every night with my nails after supper.

I was kind of moaning as well. It was a good job I wasn't seen. I'd have been certified.

Trish was on her way out. Shutting the door of her cubicle. Her face went hard at first. But then she saw I was crying and she opened the door again.

'Is it too late to say I'm sorry?'

There was a silence then. The kind of silence where

you don't know which way things are going to go. Trish started twiddling her hair. And looking around. Then she pulled me into the cubicle. Our brown and blue bark rubbings were arranged in a diamond shape over her bed.

'Look, I'm sorry, too. I know I was too hard on you. I just wish you were stronger.'

That killed me. God, there was nothing harder than making yourself sick. It was only some had the willpower.

'It takes great willpower, you know, Trish.' My voice was as stiff as hell. I couldn't go on taking the insults.

'Well, it's a pity you couldn't put it into something else. Like getting a good leaving cert to get out of here. You know that your mother will have you back here next year, if you don't do well enough.'

I don't know how Trish knew what my mother thought. Because I certainly didn't know. My guess was that she didn't care. My mother never asked me what subjects I liked. She just complained about the money she had to spend.

Maybe Trish was thinking about her own mother. But it didn't really matter because I knew what she meant. We had to get out of Mayo as quickly as possible.

'We'll get out, but what about the poor second-years and first-years?' I could still hear the groans and coughs from outside the back bathroom. And the wind was spookier there. Brenda was right.

'Look, don't mind them, it's you that's going to get really sick soon if you don't cop yourself on.'

'But poor old Brenda.'

'Poor old Brenda, my eye. That one will be fine, don't you worry. She's afraid of nothing, she doesn't believe in God.'

'I don't believe in God.'

'You only think you don't.'

I hadn't a notion of copping myself on, but I kept quiet.

'You're not really listening to me, are you? I bet you made yourself sick before you came to see me.'

'I didn't. I told Brenda it was stupid. That she didn't need to.'

'I don't think anybody needs to.' Trish's face was getting dark red and she was winding her black hair around her fingers. I was afraid that she was going to get mad again. I nearly promised to stop making myself sick.

She got up from her bed, went over to her locker and took out a photograph.

'Remember when Noreen O'Donovan was taking those photographs in study?'

'Yeah, I saw them.'

'You didn't see all of them, because I took this one out.'

I was touched at the thought of Trish hiding this photograph from me. It was vile. Huge circles scooped the skin under my eyes. Trish was next to me and looked twice as big. And twice as nice. It wasn't even the bloodshot eyes or the swollen mouth that got me, it was the expression on my face. It was dire. Scary. Lonely. Like the back bathroom. I started crying again. And Trish put her arms round me. She smelt of ink and orange skins.

We didn't talk for ages.

We didn't go back to study. We sat on the bed and after a while Trish started crying as well.

I thought I might cut down to twice a week.

'I've been so worried about you. Jesus, you've no idea how horrible it is.'

'What? Making yourself sick?'

'No, look, I wasn't going to tell you, but I think you should know, Colette killed herself.'

The walls veered at me sickeningly.

Trish grabbed me again, and held my two hands tightly in her own.

'How do you know?'

'Colette's mother came to my mother for help when it happened. I wasn't supposed to know.'

'How did it happen? Weren't they watching her all the time?'

My stomach felt cold, my hands shook. I felt hysteria in my voice. Those fools! Why didn't they watch her?

'She went downstairs in the night when they were all asleep and turned on the gas oven.'

I saw Colette with her head in the oven. Her blonde hair scattered over her thin shoulders. In her green pyjamas with the alligators. The way you could see the outline of her spine through the light material. My stomach heaved. Trish pulled me over to the sink and started splashing my face with cold water.

'Look, come on, you've got to shake out of it. And don't get sick! I'm glad I told you. You should know. Just hear me out. I don't want to protect you any more. It doesn't do you any good. Keeping you in the dark.'

We stumbled back to the bed. Trish put me under the bedclothes and got in beside me.

'She couldn't live with herself. Johnny smelt the gas and went downstairs, they rushed her to hospital, but it was too late. She left a note to say that she couldn't live like that. She had to eat and she had to vomit. She couldn't get out of the circle.'

'Don't tell me any more. I'll stop, I swear to God.'

'You don't know the half, girl. She was at it for ages and her mother knew. Mum asked her why she hadn't told the doctor and Mrs MacSweeney said it was because she couldn't cope with two children in a mental institution. Can you imagine?'

Johnny and Colette's faces were swaying over me like drunken moons. I could hardly breathe. I tried to put my hand over my mouth.

Trish tightened her grip on my hands. 'Don't you bloody get sick on me.' She went on, 'The MacSweeneys couldn't cope with it. Colette was eating raw meat and vomiting it up.'

'Raw meat?'

'Yes, this was part of the thing. She ate a lot of raw meat when she could get her hands on it. Mrs MacSweeney came back from golf early a couple of times and found Colette with her face all smeared with blood. Food all over the floor. Food and blood all over her hair. Mum said that it was a kind of primitive thing. I don't think you're like that.'

I couldn't answer.

'There's one other thing, I think this is the worst. Mrs MacSweeney used to lock Colette into her room to stop her vomiting. She'd do it anyway. And a few times she ate her own vomit so that she could vomit again.'

The walls veered in and out. Colette with her slippery fair hair covered in food and blood. Colette eating her own vomit. Colette who always smelled of Patchouli, Jasmine, Sandalwood, Franjipani or White Musk. Colette who was always having baths.

I turned into Trish and held my face against her neck.

'I've been waiting for you to come for ages.' Trish's face was fierce and flushed. She looked defiant. 'I've always been your friend. I couldn't understand why they left you in the dark. I'm sure your mother knows. Why hasn't she come to see you?'

'She's coming on Sunday.'

'About bloody time. Christ, does she ever think about you?'

'I don't think she knows how to go about it. I think she prefers my cousin.'

Trish snorted. 'Delia sounds a bit too sweet to me.'

'She's nice really, she's been good to me. Taking me out and things. She's coming on Sunday as well. You can get to meet her.'

'I'm sure I don't like her,' Trish said. I couldn't help feeling pleased.

The strange thing was I had never felt so comfortable with Trish. Even though she had told me the most terrible things. Because she had told me the most terrible things.

We didn't talk for five minutes, just lay on our backs, holding hands and staring up at the ceiling. As if there were answers up there.

We didn't hear Colm sliding the door across and only turned as her black wide shadow fell across the bed.

'Will you get back to your own bed, Grace Jones, and don't be causing disruptions.' Her voice was subdued though. As if she was under instructions. As if the convent was worried that we might all start killing ourselves. And they'd be blamed.

When I was walking back, I caught a glimpse of Colm's face. It made me think that she wished I would kill myself. 'Well, I won't,' I said to myself and threw my fully dressed body on to the bed.

She peered into my cubicle after a few minutes. I was looking at photographs of Colette.

'Don't forget to pray to your Maker. And to thank the Most Blessed Virgin that you're alive.'

After she closed the door, I got one of those awful hysterical fits of laughing that I used to get when I was with Colette. I imagined Colette saying, 'Don't forget to pray to your Maker,' in a gloomy voice.

When I got into bed and I was waiting for the sheets to heat up, I thought about Johnny. If Colette could eat raw meat, there was nothing to stop Johnny cutting Carmel's heart out. He might even eat it.

· *Thirty-four* ·

I stopped making myself sick. Kind of. I still gave in to it every now and then. When I was fed up with crying. The less I got sick the more I cried. As if getting sick had been some kind of crying. Through my mouth and stomach.

It mortified me. Having to give way to fits of crying all the time. In front of first-years. Their wondering faces. It attracted Carmel's attention and I didn't want that. That made me even more guilty. Waiting for Johnny.

Every now and then I thought about telling Trish. But I never did.

Trish and I drew two huge pictures of The Cell, it took us a week to colour them in and then we hung them over our beds like they were pictures of the Sacred Heart.

'Is it modern art?' Carmel asked when she saw them. She didn't ask us to take them down.

We had this plan to draw a giant tree with red apples. We were going to put an important list inside each apple. The characteristics of living things or the constituents of the blood. The different phases of a heart beat.

I moaned slightly thinking about Carmel and Johnny.

We decided to do the apples first. I couldn't get the shape right. I spent one whole night in study rubbing at crooked pencil curves.

'It won't come right if you think about it,' Trish said and made gallant sweeps with her pencil.

One morning at breaktime, one of the day girls handed me a note: '*I'll be at the farm. Four o'clock.*'

I thought that it was a real criminal note. No signature. No sweet nothings. Clinically cold. Like a calculated killing. I could hardly hear myself talk above the beating of my heart.

I went for a walk with Trish after lunch, I was going to tell her except my stomach was too heavy. She'd made me eat a giant potato and I was fighting the urge to get rid of it.

Carmel had smiled at me as I left the refectory. Sad. Like it was her last smile. And still I looked forward to Johnny's eyes slanting at me. The thin wicked-looking roll up between his fingers. Oh God, the way he looked at me!

I began to think that hell might exist. Just when the Catholic church was trying to phase it out.

At lunchtime, Trish made me race her round the walks, she was talking about building up my muscles. I wasn't keen, but I pretended to be mad for it because I didn't want her to notice how jittery I was.

Last class was free, since I'd given up honours Irish. At half past three I went to sit in the cloister with my French verb book. Not that I gave one damn about French verbs. I just didn't want to be drawing attention to myself with a novel.

My hair was in two plaits over my ears. I'd had a bit

of agonising over them, but I decided I was better with my hair away from my face. What if it blew across my mouth at a crucial moment? The farm was fiercely windy.

I loved the smooth stone floor of the cloister, I let my shoes slide along. They made whispery whistle sounds as they went. Then I pulled myself together. The last thing I wanted was being sent up to the study and getting stuck with Trish or Brenda or something.

The darkening sky made the cloister a grey tunnel, little pin pricks of rain began to tinkle on the glass roof. They got harder and stronger, rivulets poured down the walls. My heart fell down. Fucking rain.

Jesus! Why was I being tormented?

I started reading my French verbs like they were prayers. *Je donnerais, Je donnerais, Je donnerais,* I got stuck at the very first one. Why did they need so many bloody tenses? Wasn't past, present and future enough for them? It was too much for me.

I sensed her coming before I heard her scratchy nylon housecoat.

'Sister Carmel!'

'Grace! What are you doing here in the dark! You'll ruin your eyes.'

'Is it dark?' I started guiltily, looking at the wet purple sky through the glass roof.

She put her small hand on the light switch and the corridor flooded with light. She had a black raincoat over her arm.

'Where are you going, Sister Carmel?'

'I've had an urgent message.' Carmel dived one of her small round arms into the sleeve of her black raincoat.

'From where?' I insisted.

Carmel stared at my hands, I looked down and saw the way I was wringing and squeezing my French verbs.

'Sorry,' I said stupidly and tried to smooth the cover.

Carmel slid the rest of herself into the black raincoat, it reached down to her toes. I noticed that she was wearing wellingtons. My heart got fierce loud.

'Are you going to the farm?' I asked, trying to sound casual.

'Well, how did you guess?' Carmel patted my shoulder. 'Sometimes I think you can read my mind. Oh those innocent eyes!'

Can you imagine the knife twisting inside me? I stood there, my hands snaking around my French verbs, even my tongue felt forked.

'Don't go, Sister!'

'Grace, calm down. I have to go. Sister Antonio is waiting above with a sick calf.' Carmel waved a brown bottle of medicine at me.

'It's a lie, it's a trick, can't you see?'

'What is wrong with you, Grace?' Carmel put her rough hand on my forehead.

'Did Sister Antonio speak to you directly? Did you hear it from her lips?'

Carmel's forehead went into furrows.

I clung on to her black raincoat. 'You mustn't go, it's a matter of life or death.'

Her wellingtons shifted uneasily.

'Grace, I'm not letting you out in the rain, and I'm not letting Antonio down. If you continue on like this, I'll have to call Mother Colm to take you to the infirmary.'

Carmel shook off my hand and went to the door.

'I'm sorry, Grace, but this is important. Think of the poor little calf. We'll have a nice chat in the refectory when I get back.'

I let her go ahead a few minutes and then I ran out. It was four o'clock now. I was afraid she'd look back but she didn't. I was drenched after about three minutes, but I kept going. I wondered if I could be seen from the kitchen windows. I was sure there had never been anything so suspicious-looking as my long-coated figure darting at a distance behind Sister Carmel.

At the farm, Carmel quickly disappeared into some sheds. I bit my tongue with anxiety. And then Johnny grabbed my arm.

At least he wasn't waiting for her in the sheds.

He pulled me into the milking parlour. His wet head looked smaller than I remembered. He smelt of cider or some sweet kind of drink.

'Will we have a fag?' he asked. Cool as anything.

I couldn't believe it, but then I realised he was playing innocent.

'Okay,' I said, bidding for time.

Johnny took a tin box out of his pocket.

'I don't take drugs,' I said stiffly. I was annoyed too because I had wanted to try some. But now I had to keep my wits about me. I had to put Carmel first.

'You must think I'm made of money! I don't have dope at every drop of the hat you know!'

I didn't think our meeting was the drop of a hat. But I said nothing. I had to think of Sister Carmel's safety.

Then I had to tell him that I couldn't roll cigarettes which was a bit humiliating. He said that he didn't mind.

We leaned against a stall and he put his arm round my shoulder. Loosely. Not like the iron bands he'd put round me at Colette's funeral.

I waited to feel ravished or mystical, but nothing happened. I thought I might have an even bigger potato for my supper.

I felt cheated and dragged on my cigarette. The

tobacco went all over my tongue. Roll ups seemed small and mean suddenly. Cheap. I swallowed the tobacco. Not to spare Johnny's feelings but because I didn't want to make a show of myself.

I took another pull from the cigarette and got a huge mouthful of tobacco. I wondered what Carmel was doing as I secretly examined my cigarette which was disintegrating into shreds of paper and stringy tobacco.

'You've made a duck's arse out of that.' Johnny grabbed it out of my hand and ground it out on the cement floor with the heel of his big boot.

'You're so fucking innocent.' He smiled at me. Indulgent. Pulling me into his arms.

Innocent? I was dying from intrigue. My heart was failing from my double life.

Then he kissed me.

Mystical.

I forgot about the big potato.

If he'd only just kept kissing me on the lips it would have been okay, but he tried to put his tongue between my teeth.

He touched my tongue. My forked tongue!

I knew Carmel was there then, standing in the doorway. I didn't hear the scratching, I just felt it like it was inside my chest. Pushing me away from Johnny.

My face was hot and red, I shoved at Johnny. I was so savage.

At first I was mortified that she'd seen us kissing. Tongues and everything. Really disgusting.

But then I remembered.

'Carmel, he's dangerous. Run while you can!'

Carmel just stood there with her pink cheeks gone pale. Or maybe it was the white walls of the milking parlour that were draining her.

'Please go!' I ran across to try and touch her, but I

slid on the wet cement floor. My heart lowered and went cold. Like falling in a dream. I skidded to a halt in front of her small wellingtons. They had black roundy toes. Demure. Like they were specially made for nuns.

It seemed like only a small twist to the ankle, but when I tried to get up, I gasped and fell down again.

Johnny picked up the tin box which had fallen on its side.

Carmel had her arm round me then. 'What are you doing to her?'

'I did nothing, I swear to God!' Johnny put his hands above his head, trying to be light-hearted.

My ankle seared, it blew up under my eyes. 'He has made threats against you.'

'It was only a joke.'

Johnny looked stupid. I was going right off him.

The only thing was that I felt even more stupid.

Carmel didn't look mortally scared. But she did look awful sorry for us.

'You'll have to help me get her down to the school, and if we're seen by Sister Paul, she might get expelled.' Carmel's mouth was really mean-looking when she spoke to Johnny. 'You're old enough to know you shouldn't be putting Grace in danger. She's too innocent for the likes of you!'

My forked tongue shifted uneasily in my mouth. I felt bad for Johnny. Imagine having Carmel giving out to you! I wanted to explain that he was on *lithium*. That he couldn't help himself.

Johnny carried me down to the school and he never complained or said that I was a sack of potatoes.

He shook Carmel's hand outside the cloister and my heart was as swollen as my ankle. I knew that I could never have anything to do with him again as long as I was at Mayo. Because I could never risk Carmel getting caught out by Paul. If it ever got back that she had covered up for us, they'd kill her.

It was only when he'd turned away that I noticed that he was wearing new Levis. They were still stiff and boardy looking. Fierce sad. And the way his head looked so small when it was wet.

My lower lip was going when Carmel helped me into the bed.

'It's all over now.' She was desperate firm. 'I'll do you a poached egg on toast.'

'*It's all over now.*'

Scratch, scratch went her black nylon housecoat.

'*Baby blue,*' I said and she looked at me.

The tears came like rain on the cloister.

· *Thirty-five* ·

The worst part was waking up morning after morning. Realising that I wasn't in love with Johnny. There was no one exciting left to think about.

After a few days I got used to it. My ankle got better, I hobbled around. One thing bothered me though. The day girls had seen Johnny hanging around town. Apparently he was staying with the hippies.

Then one morning Carmel came to call me and she was very distracted. 'Oh, I'm glad you're awake. I can't stop, Grace, I'm in a terrible hurry. There's been an incident, Sister Peter is gone into shock. Pray for her!'

She slid the door shut before I could ask her what had happened. I washed quickly and was trying to get my tie in a straight knot when Trish came.

'How did you sleep?' I asked.

Trish looked awful pale.

'Not great, I've been thinking about Colette.'

'So have I,' *and Johnny*, I added mentally.

'It's really sinking in now.'

'What is?'

'That she's dead.'

I hated having to think about it.

I was worn out from crying. And making myself sick. Everything was so tiring.

There was another knock.

'I suppose we'll never get rid of you,' Trish said to Brenda.

'No,' said Brenda and sat down on the bed, really brazen.

My tie had got even more crooked. Trish fixed it. I looked in the mirror at Brenda. The way she was lying on my bed, with her eyes half closed, reminded me of Colette.

At Mass, you could see there was something wrong. The prayers from the nuns' chapel were louder and even more fervent than usual. Paul's pale face was grim and several of the nuns looked as if they had been crying. At the very end, when all the other nuns had had their communion, Carmel helped Sister Peter up to the rails. She had a shawl over her head and her tongue seemed to be shaking as she held it out for the communion.

At breakfast in the refectory, Colm was like a savage. She said Grace Before Meals, throwing out the words like she was stoning us.

'There's definitely something up,' said Trish.

Nobody knew what it was. But, then, we saw Noreen O'Donovan going off with Colm.

'Follow them,' Trish told Brenda.

I had two slices of brown bread for breakfast. Then I wished that I hadn't, my stomach felt too full. I wanted to get sick. In the dormitory afterwards, my fingers kept creeping into my mouth. Like secret mice that were programmed.

But I didn't. The idea of being healthy was kind of attractive. Having no dark circles on my cheeks and being able to run round the walks in the evening. Not *having* to kneel down in front of the toilet every single evening. And not being exhausted all the time. I thought that I might buy a box of All Bran next time I went to confession. Get healthy.

Then I saw Johnny. I was standing at the big window in Saint Joseph's, thinking about Colette, picturing her head in the gas oven. Over and over. Suddenly, I saw him come out of the woods where the stream was, and go running down the side path that led to the farm. A few minutes later, Paul came from the convent and stared into the woods. She stayed like that for a while and then walked back into the convent, shaking her fist slightly. She seemed to be talking to herself.

Noreen O'Donovan had the whole story for us at breaktime. A man had exposed himself to Sister Peter in the woods after supper the previous evening. Peter was so bad after it that she had to get a special injection. The nuns had searched the woods but they couldn't find him. The Guards had been called, too, but were completely useless, according to Colm.

Sister Peter had described a young slight man with a skinhead haircut. The Guard taking the notes had thrown his head back, laughed and said the town was full of them. It was after the Guard laughed that Peter had to get the injection. According to Colm, the Guards had spent no time searching the woods. And had rushed off in the squad car when it started raining.

I told Trish that I'd seen Johnny.

'I thought it might be him. I had a feeling that he was around. He's after you, I think,' Trish snorted as if this was desperate funny. And of course Brenda had to laugh too.

I didn't see what was so funny. 'But Johnny wouldn't do a thing like that?'

'Expose himself?'

'Yes.'

'You never know with mad people. He mightn't be responsible for himself.'

I was going off Johnny anyway, but I couldn't bear the thought that I'd been kissing a flasher. That I'd allowed him to put his knee between my knees.

'Ah, come on, Trish. I'm sure he's not that mad.'

'He bloody well is.'

'Maybe he was going to the loo,' Brenda said.

'Yes, that must be it.' I gave Brenda a wild grateful look.

'Possible,' said Trish, pursing her lips.

I had an awful feeling that Trish knew about me and Johnny, that she was teasing. But I wasn't sure and I was determined not to fall into any traps.

As the day wore on, I was getting more and more nervous about suppertime. I wished I didn't have to eat. It was a strange day, very gloomy in the refectory. Carmel hardly spoke to me. She was worried about Peter.

Brenda didn't have any sympathy for Peter, 'Peter grew up on a farm, she must have seen them before.'

'Seen what?'

'Oh you know what I mean.'

'It was probably the skinhead haircut and the mad eyes,' Trish said, laying a heavy emphasis on the word mad.

At suppertime I hardly ate.

Trish raised her eyebrows at me.

'I don't want to feel too full,' I said. 'Then I won't be able to stop myself.'

'That's useless then,' said Trish. 'You can't have it ruling your life.'

So I had two slices of brown bread with strawberry jam. I nearly enjoyed them, the bread was so fresh.

'Good girl,' said Carmel, half absentmindedly, passing by.

Sister Peter had got up and was washing stainless-steel dish covers at the top of the refectory.

Just before Carmel said Grace After Meals the refectory door flew open and Paul burst in with the megaphone.

'Right. Now. I want every girl here to say a silent prayer for poor Sister Peter who's lying above in the convent next door to unconsciousness,' Paul screeched on the megaphone.

Everyone looked at Peter who was holding a dish cover up to the light. Checking to see if she was shining it right.

Paul couldn't fail to see our heads turning and she followed our eyes.

'Ah, you're there, Sister Peter! Soldiering on.'

Peter waved the dish cover vaguely.

'Right, I'm sure every girl here has heard of the shocking incident that happened to Sister Peter last night.'

Paul looked at Peter again. You could see that it was putting her off, having Peter there polishing the dish covers. She couldn't let herself go.

'Now, I'm very sorry to say and with all due respect we've been let down badly by the *Garda Siochana*. Perhaps they're overstressed with the crimes of modern life. We don't know. But we cannot allow this lurking about the convent woods to go on. I'm calling on every girl here and it's every girl's Christian duty to follow Mother Colm and myself outside where we intend to run the culprit to ground.'

Paul took a few quick breaths then and turned to Carmel. 'You may go on with the Grace now, Sister Carmel.'

We joined our hands and Carmel said the Grace. I

thought that she was saying it a bit slow. As if she wanted to put off the terrible moment when we all had to go out and run the culprit to ground.

Trish was bursting her sides. Brenda was killing herself. I was mortified. If I hadn't kissed him in the milking parlour, maybe he wouldn't have stayed around.

As we were filing out of the refectory, I tried to dodge off to the dormitory, but Colm barred the way, directing everyone to the cloakroom.

'Every single girl is to wear her gaberdine coat with the hood up and belt it tightly.'

Brenda was with us again in the cloakroom and her face looked tiny, peering out of the huge bottle-green hood.

'Aren't you deserting your friends?' I asked her. I couldn't help noticing the bad looks I was getting from the second-years, especially Brenda's friend Geraldine White.

'All they ever talk about is food.'

'All Trish and I ever do is fight,' I said, hoping that she would contradict me.

'Ah, but it's exciting,' said Brenda, pushing her red curls back into the hood.

Outside, we gathered in front of the statue of Saint Gabriel. It was half drizzling. 'It's fierce cold,' Brenda said, folding her arms tightly.

'Has she gone stone mad?' Trish thrust her hands into the pockets of her gaberdine.

Paul had put on a huge cape raincoat. It flew back in the wind behind her marbly face and neck.

'If I was Johnny, I'd be shaking in my shoes,' whispered Trish.

Paul turned up the megaphone and it screeched and whistled.

'Get into ranks,' came Paul's mangled voice.

We looked at each other in amazement.

'Form yourselves into lines,' barked Colm.

'Line up according to your year,' trumpeted Paul's voice from the megaphone. 'Leaving certs to form the vanguard.'

Brenda got separated from us then.

We were driven across the woods with Paul roaring into the amplifier behind us, 'Fan out, fan out.'

We stumbled this way and that, but we hadn't a clue and Paul kept shouting, 'Come out if you're man enough!' and 'Give up now, we have you surrounded!'

'Jesus, I wouldn't come out if I was man enough.'

I tried not to slip on the ground which had gone slimy with the rain. My ankle wasn't completely cured and I began to hobble a bit. I was surprised that nobody noticed it. Not even Trish.

Paul kept it up for ages and then, when we thought that she was giving up, she found a cigarette packet.

'Onward, onward, we're on your trail, punk.'

We didn't know where she got the word punk, she must have read it in the paper. She kept shouting it, over and over, and the first-years were having heart attacks laughing. Colm was the rearguard. She looked as grim and as sour as ever. Noreen O'Donovan said Colm was too old for it and she was afraid of falling.

'Isn't Paul too old for it as well?' asked Trish.

My only comfort was that I had seen Johnny going up to the farm and he was probably far away by now.

In the end, one of the first-years fell and another one lost her shoe. The search was called off.

'We've got your number, punk!' shouted Paul, in one last defiant roar into the megaphone, before swinging around in her big black cape and leading us all back into the cloister.

Carmel opened up the refectory again and everyone

got a cup of cocoa. We hardly had time to drink it, though, before Colm was hustling us back up the stairs. We were to go to bed early.

Noreen O'Donovan was furious. 'I was going to revise the second world war!' she hissed at Colm.

'Go up to your dormitory, Noreen and don't be cheeky,' said Colm.

A couple of girls tried to have baths, but they were driven back to the dormitory by Colm.

'Is it to have baths, when there's a man loose in the grounds of the school? Have you got no common decency at all? Get back up the stairs and cover yourselves immediately!'

The two girls got into bed and didn't even try to wash themselves.

The rest of us were half undressed, when the lights went out.

'Get into bed, every girl!' Paul's voice screeched from the megaphone.

I had my leg in the washbasin. I took it out and stood, dripping.

'Who knows when he'll come back! It's every girl's duty to protect her modesty. Get into bed now, you can say your prayers under the covers. God will understand.'

She banged the door shut and I could hear girls relaxing and trying to find their way into their beds in the dark. Then the door opened again and another cry pierced out of the megaphone across the dormitory.

'And don't forget to pray for the soul of Sister Peter!'

After a while Trish came in and sat on my bed.

We figured that Peter couldn't be dead. She'd looked fine when she was polishing the dish covers.

· *Thirty-six* ·

I was sick of crying and I couldn't make myself sick, so I decided to take up smoking again. I sent down to the town for French cigarettes. *Gitane.*

One of the town girls put them into my folder. All day during classes, I peered into the folder, admiring the packet. My favourite deep blue. And the swirly woman's black outline was sophisticated and worldly. Like when I got out of school and got away from my mother. Brilliant.

I gave Brenda and Trish the slip and sneaked up to the back attic. I sat on a roll of old linoleum and took out the packet. I rustled the cellophane for a few minutes, sliding it around the flat box. Then I pulled the thin red strip and the clear wrapping fell away in two slippery boxes.

'Freedom!' I said and took out my box of red matches. I had especially asked for red ones because I liked the way that they rasped.

But it was a while since I'd smoked and I didn't know how strong French cigarettes were. I took a desperate deep drag and nearly keeled over. I righted myself, though, and kept smoking. Half way through the cigarette, I had to admit that it wasn't the sensation

I'd been hoping for. And then I felt hungry. Putting out the cigarette carefully, I squeezed it back into the box with the other ones. The cigarettes looked so nice in a row. Short and fat. All white. Like sticks of chalk. They didn't have that light brown paper on the filter end. Like ordinary cigarettes had.

It was a pity I didn't like them.

I decided to go to the refectory and get some bread. Look for Trish. The cigarette packet didn't fit into my pocket so I put it up my sleeve. I went to the back door that led to the back stairs. The steps were really steep before you got to the third floor and they frightened me. I was always frightened of falling down the stairs. I remembered my dream about Colette the night before Carmel told me that she was dead.

Once I got to the third floor, I felt safe and I ran quickly down the back stairs past the blue bathroom. The sound of coughing and spluttering made me stop and listen. Someone was running the tap. I wanted to keep going but I listened in spite of myself. Some girl muttering to herself. She sounded familiar. This embarrassed me. I didn't want to bump into whoever it was and I hurried my steps. As I went past, the door was flung suddenly open. I looked back.

It was Brenda. Her thin skin covered in red blotches, her eyes bloodshot.

'Brenda! What are you doing?' I ran up the stairs and I would have shaken her except that I suddenly couldn't bear to touch her.

She stood staring at me, looking wild. A bit mad. My heart missed a beat. I thought of Colette and Johnny.

'It's no good, I can't do it! I've tried and I've tried. I drank salty water with two spoons of mustard. No good.' She began to weep and threw herself onto my chest. She was light and limp.

I put my arms round her. 'If you made yourself sick, I'd kill you. Except I wouldn't be able to touch you.'

'I wanted to, so much. I've got a fierce pain in my throat, I think it's haemorrhaging.'

'Don't be stupid! What made you do it?'

'You!'

'But I *told* you it was really stupid. You've no freedom. It's like prison, except you're stuck in a toilet all the time.'

'You just don't want to be my friend. What's the point of anything?'

'Jesus, Brenda, I can't believe the drama! You're trying to blackmail me.'

'Well, not anymore,' Brenda sobbed, and pawed at a sodden tissue. 'I've failed to do it.' She ran her thin-skinned pink fingers through her curly hair and looked at me. 'But you do like me. You know you do. You're just too chicken to admit it.'

'I'm not too chicken. I do like you. But leaving certs don't hang around with second-years.'

'See! You are chicken, you're afraid of what people will think.'

'It's not just that. You give me no space. I need time on my own.'

'Well, just let me collect you for Mass in the mornings.'

'I'll think about it,' I said.

'Ah do! Please think about it.'

'I don't see why you're getting so excited. I'll be gone at the end of the year. The second-years mightn't want you back then.'

'The second-years want only to get sick and anyway I'll be gone at the end of the year too.'

'How do you mean?'

'My mother's taking me out, I'm starting at day school next year. I've got a place in St Jo's.'

'Why is your mother taking you out?'

'She says that it's a desperate place, that we're being repressed.'

'She sounds nice.'

'She's fierce nice.'

Maybe it was because Brenda had a brilliant mother and I was hoping that some of that good mothering would rub off on me, but I agreed to be her friend. And to let her collect me for Mass. I said that if she ever attempted to make herself sick again, I'd cut off all contact. She said that she'd do the same if I made myself sick, and that took me back a bit.

'*And* I'll report you to Paul,' I said. Really savage about the way she got the better of me when I least expected it.

'I'm supposed to believe that, am I?' Brenda wrinkled up her nose and looked about fifty-five.

'You believed it last year when I stopped you from having that midnight feast in the Little Flower.'

'Jesus, yeah! You were really bossy and my mother was going to bring in cooked sausages and everything.'

'Was she? What kind?'

'Little cocktail sausages and sausage rolls and a roast chicken.'

My mouth watered thinking about sausage rolls. The soft flakes of pastry and the picnicky taste. Roast chicken! Real food. Not like the greasy overcooked smelly refectory food.

'And would your mother bring in the food?'

'She'd be only too delighted.'

'Why did she send you here?'

'It was just to please old Sister Benedicta, you know we're related? I mean Benedicta's fierce nice and everything, but she's blind as a bat and she's got nothing to do with the school. My mother rues the day she sent me here.'

'Why?'

'I'm telling you she says we're repressed and anyway I've told her all about the second-years getting sick.'

I was thinking about sage and onion stuffing. 'How far away do you live?'

'Only twelve miles.'

'And she'd drive here with all that stuff?'

'Are you thinking of having one?'

'Yes,' I said and I wasn't scared any more. If they expelled me, I'd only have to stick my mother for another six months then I'd have left school.

'Let's have it down by the stream.' I could feel myself swelling as I took things into my own hands. 'We'll be able to sneak out the cloister door after ten o'clock. The nuns will all be meditating in the convent.'

'How do you know that?' Brenda asked.

'I just know,' I said, feeling a bit of a twinge because it was Carmel who had told me.

'We'll have it in the dead of night,' Brenda said and frightened herself into a shivering fit.

'We're going to have to plan it seriously,' I said. 'Make lists.'

'And diagrams,' Trish said when we told her about it.

The evening before the midnight feast, Brenda's mother arrived with a cooked chicken, cocktail sausages, sausage rolls and a massive rectangle of gingerbread. I didn't get to see her, but Trish did. Trish said that she was really brilliant.

'She doesn't give a shit!'

I clasped my hands just thinking about her. I didn't want to give a shit either. I kept thinking about leaving school.

Brenda kept the chicken and the sausages under her

bed. Trish and I bought crisps and chocolate at Colm's tuck shop.

'Oh, we're eating now, are we?' Colm said, looking me up and down like mad.

I kept my face neutral, because I didn't want her to suspect there was anything.

'Jesus! Why did you look so guilty?' Trish exclaimed as we were walking away.

We raided the kitchen after lights out. That was the scariest. The kitchens were old and eerie and I felt bad about Carmel.

Trish hacked slices of ham off a big joint in the pantry and I filled my emptied physics folder with cheese and slices of soda bread. We found a big box of marshmallow biscuits and filled our pockets with them. Brenda sat on the huge kitchen table and shook a cannister of cornflakes.

'Cop on,' Trish hissed. 'They'll be all crushed.' We were going to sprinkle corn flakes on mashed banana. Trish said that it was really brilliant, but only if you ate it with your fingers.

'So that's how you got all those greasy paw marks on your biology book,' Brenda said.

'What were you doing looking at my biology book?'

'I didn't realise that it was yours. It was on Grace's desk.'

'And what are you doing poking around *my* desk? I could have private letters or anything.'

'No, I couldn't find any private letters.' Brenda looked so disappointed Trish and I couldn't stop laughing.

But when I was finished laughing, I told her I didn't want her to do it again. I wondered if my strict face was as bad as my neutral face.

We wore jeans under our uniforms and two jumpers under our gabardines and we weren't a bit cold. We spread blankets down by the river. Trish and Brenda ate like mad.

'No fear of you getting anorexia,' I said to Brenda. Just to annoy her.

I couldn't eat a pile of stuff, but I had two sausage rolls, gingerbread and some chicken breast that Brenda made me eat. I put a load of salt on my chicken and we were licking our fingers for ages after we'd finished eating.

The sky was a very dark blue and it had really swirly clouds blocking out the moon. Trish said it was just like something Vincent Van Gogh would throw down on a bit of paper.

Brenda wanted me to tell a ghost story but I wouldn't. I told her it was punishment for poking around my desk.

'Where did you put the torch?' she asked. 'I've brought something that I want to read.'

I gave her the torch and she turned it on. It shone on a library book.

'What is it?'

'*Frankenstein.*'

'You're not going to read it to us, are you?' Trish asked as she sprinkled salt on a crispy bit of chicken skin.

'Look, I've been practising. I've decided to become an actress.'

'Go on,' I said. It was ages since I'd read *Frankenstein.*

'It was a dreary night of November, that I beheld the accomplishment of my toils,' Brenda's voice was good. She didn't exaggerate too much and that made it more scary.

The moon was sliding in and out of the clouds like mad and there was a warm breeze. Brenda read, '. . . by the glimmer of the half extinguished light, I saw the dull yellow eye of the creature open; it breathed hard, and a convulsive motion agitated its limbs.

'I can't do it any more,' Brenda put her arms around me and buried her head on my shoulder.

'The nuns' graveyard is only round the corner,' Trish teased Brenda.

I grabbed the book with my left hand and focussed the torch with my right. It was a bit hard to do with Brenda lying all over me, but I swept on, 'How can I describe my emotions at this catastrophe . . .'

Brenda couldn't stop saying *Jesus.*

'I thought that you were an atheist,' Trish said.

'It's my father's the atheist, not me,' Brenda said, but she sat up properly and watched the words over my shoulder.

I heard my voice floating like a ghost, it made me feel different and I put the book down.

I walked away on my own and stood staring at another part of the stream. Where it bent and disappeared under a pile of trees.

Making yourself sick was like making Frankenstein's monster. Trying to control nature and then getting chased by your own monster. I didn't want to spend the rest of my life running into toilets. Staring at taps and tiles while I was psyching myself up. Getting to know every crack in every wall. Staring at chrome.

I was going to try to be natural. Like greasy fingers. The smell of chicken. The sound of the water on the stones in the stream and the swish of the wind in the trees.

It wasn't going to be easy. Trying to be natural. It was like the future. Fairly spooky. Maybe brilliant.

Also available from Mandarin Paperbacks

CAROL BIRCH

Songs of the West

'In Carol Birch's skilful novel, prosperous foreign incomers to furthest south-west Ireland buy large houses and establish "affirmation centres", make yoghurt and criticise commercialism. Meanwhile, the local country people get on with earning a living. Essie, middle-class and English, with seventeen rings in her ears and a stud in her tongue, makes earthenware knick-knacks. Rosanna is an anarchic alcoholic. Their friend Marie is a respectable wife and mother. One summer Marie falls for a writer from Dublin who passes through in his yellow caravan . . . Carol Birch writes beautifully about a place she must know and love, and has an acute ear for dialogue'
Sunday Telegraph

'Full of richly imagined characters, written with a fluent assurance'
Sunday Times

'*Songs of the West* is extremely hard to put aside . . . it is good to read the work of a writer who looks and listens so closely'
Times Literary Supplement

'Bustles with characters . . . a rich, often funny novel'
New Statesman

A Selected List of Fiction Available from Mandarin

While every effort is made to keep prices low, it is sometimes necessary to increase prices at short notice. Mandarin Paperbacks reserves the right to show new retail prices on covers which may differ from those previously advertised in the text or elsewhere.

The prices shown below were correct at the time of going to press.

☐	7493 1352 8	**The Queen and I**	Sue Townsend	£5.99
☐	7493 1683 7	**Adrian Mole: The Wilderness Years**	Sue Townsend	£4.99
☐	7493 0540 1	**The Liar**	Steven Fry	£5.99
☐	7493 2233 0	**The Gobbler**	Adrian Edmondson	£5.99
☐	7493 1132 0	**Arrivals and Departures**	Leslie Thomas	£5.99
☐	7493 1888 0	**Running Away**	Leslie Thomas	£4.99
☐	7493 0054 X	**The Silence of the Lambs**	Thomas Harris	£5.99
☐	7493 0946 6	**The Godfather**	Mario Puzo	£5.99
☐	7493 1477 X	**The Name of the Rose**	Umberto Eco	£5.99
☐	7493 1319 6	**Air and Angels**	Susan Hill	£6.99
☐	7493 1930 5	**Hemingway's Chair**	Michael Palin	£5.99
☐	7493 1518 0	**The Ex-Wives**	Deborah Moggach	£5.99
☐	7493 2014 1	**Changing Babies**	Deborah Moggach	£5.99
☐	7493 2034 6	**The Bridges of Madison County**	Robert James Waller	£4.99
☐	7493 2310 8	**Border Music**	Robert James Waller	£4.99

All these books are available at your bookshop or newsagent, or can be ordered direct from the address below. Just tick the titles you want and fill in the form below.

Cash Sales Department, PO Box 5, Rushden, Northants NN10 6YX.
Fax: 01933 414047 : Phone: 01933 414000.

Please send cheque, payable to 'Reed Book Services Ltd.', or postal order for purchase price quoted and allow the following for postage and packing:

£1.00 for the first book, 50p for the second; **FREE POSTAGE AND PACKING FOR THREE BOOKS OR MORE PER ORDER.**

NAME (Block letters)..

ADDRESS..

....

☐ I enclose my remittance for..........................

☐ I wish to pay by Access/Visa Card Number ☐☐☐☐☐☐☐☐☐☐☐☐☐☐☐☐

Expiry Date ☐☐☐☐

Signature..

Please quote our reference: MAND